HAUNTED
SWEETS

Connie Shelton

HAUNTED SWEETS

Samantha Sweet Mysteries, Book 17

Connie Shelton

Secret Staircase Books

Haunted Sweets
Published by Secret Staircase Books, an imprint of
Columbine Publishing Group, LLC
PO Box 416, Angel Fire, NM 87710

Book layout and design by Secret Staircase Books
Cover images © Makeitdoubleplz, BooksRMe

First trade paperback edition: October 2023
First e-book edition: October 2023
* * *

Publisher's Cataloging-in-Publication Data

Shelton, Connie
Haunted Sweets / by Connie Shelton.
p. cm.
ISBN 978-1649141484 (paperback)
ISBN 978-1649141491 (e-book)

1. Samantha Sweet (Fictitious character)--Fiction. 2. Taos, New
Mexico—Fiction. 3. Paranormal activity—Fiction. 4. Bakery—
Fiction. 5. Women sleuths—Fiction. I. Title

Samantha Sweet Mystery Series : Book 17.
Shelton, Connie, Samantha Sweet mysteries.

BISAC : FICTION / Mystery & Detective.
813/.54

To Dan, always.

Chapter 1

Samantha Sweet put the final touch on the flourless truffle cakes on her worktable. Twenty-five perfect little triangles of rich-enough-to-die-for chocolate, topped with a fresh Melba sauce and each with a dollop of whipped cream. Now that the weather had cooled a bit and the wedding season was nearly over, Sam found herself gravitating toward richer recipes and the heavier fare that autumn dictated.

"Does Ivan need all of those for the meeting?" her daughter asked, barely keeping the whimper out of her voice.

"Well, Kelly, no he does not. In fact, the mystery book club is down to eight or ten members, and I'd planned on sending enough for each to take two …"

"So, maybe there would be one or two for me to take home?"

"Maybe." Sam gave her daughter a wink and set three of the pastries into a box. "There's no way I'm leaving either Scott or Anastasia out of the deal."

"I give a five-year-old one of those and she'll be bouncing off the walls at midnight. She gets half, or maybe two bites."

Sam laughed at the description of her very energetic and precocious granddaughter. "No kidding. Just because they're flourless doesn't mean they're sugarless. A couple bites should be good."

Kelly took one of the pastries out of the box and placed it in a separate, fresh one. "I owe Emily a peace offering. I cancelled our get-together this afternoon."

"What happened?" Sam set the sticky saucepan into the sink, dodging Julio, her head baker.

"She'd asked me to help sort through another box of documents in her grandfather's collection. I mean, I love reading about the history of Taos, and her granddad really did find some amazing things. It's just that Scott hasn't taken a day off from his writing schedule all month, and he goes on tour in a few days with the new book … I just felt like we needed family time more than Em needed a fellow paper-sorter. I bailed on her."

"I get that. It wasn't the wrong call."

"I don't think so either. But I also feel guilty as anything. So, I'm going to take her one of these. And the minute Scott locks himself away in his writing room, I'll pop by the library and offer it to her along with my services for a few hours of delving into the past. What do you think?"

"Perfect." Sam boxed the rest of the chocolate cakes, knowing Ivan Petrenko would be over within the hour to pick them up. He'd mentioned having a visiting author this month for the meeting of mystery book discussion and indulgence. The group called themselves Chocoholics Unanimous for a reason.

"Okay, then. I'm off. We're taking Ana to the new Pixar movie and then it's pizza and wings for Scott's portion of the program."

"And your part? What's Kelly's special treat?"

Her daughter held up the box with the cakes, waggling it with an almost-seductive smile.

"You'd better get home so you can begin the day's festivities," Sam teased.

The bells at the front door tinkled in the background, and Sam heard Ivan's voice as he greeted Jen at the front counter. Kelly ducked out the back with her bounty, and Sam carried the boxed truffle cakes out front.

"Ah, Miss Sam, is being good to see you!" greeted the enthusiastic Russian immigrant. Sam had never quite pieced together his history and doubted she ever would. Mainly, she knew he loved books, and his shop next door to hers was one of the most successful in town.

She held up the box, with the lid open, so he could inspect her latest creation. The Chocoholics didn't much care what she made for their monthly meeting, only that it be decadent and chocolate. Occasionally, Ivan would give her a hint and she would design something to fit the theme of the book they were reading, but this time he'd given no clues.

"Who's the visiting author you mentioned?" she asked as she accepted the check he handed over.

"Susan Slater. Amazing writer. She lives in Albuquerque. Started career as protégée of Tony Hillerman." His eyes were wide.

"So, she writes similar? Mysteries with Indian themes?"

"And more. Of course, we focus on her newest Ben Pecos book for the group this month. But she also writes a Florida mystery series, and a few standing-alone books. My customers, they love them all. You should come."

"What time?"

"Meeting at three. Cake at four," he said as she held the door for him.

"I'll see if I can break away."

Two wedding cakes later, Sam breathed a sigh. The four-tier ivory buttercream one needed a few small touches, and Becky could handle those. The two-tier with pale pink fondant and deep dusty-rose flowers was ready and would be picked up by the customer later this afternoon. She looked at the clock above the bake ovens. The book club event at Ivan's was well underway, but she could manage to tiptoe in and get the chance to meet the bestselling author. She hung up her baker's jacket, washed her hands, and headed next door.

When she walked into the familiar bookshop, it was to a riot of raucous laughter, and she paused half a second in the doorway. But the book club members, seated in their neat semi-circle facing the author's table weren't looking in Sam's direction at all. Every eye was tuned to the woman with the dark pixie-cut hair and glasses with red frames who'd apparently just finished reading a passage from her book. A fairly bawdy passage, if Sam judged the blush on Ivan's face correctly.

"That comes from my newest work in progress," the

author announced. "And from your reaction, I'd say it works."

"You said the new one is somewhat biographical?" one of the ladies in the audience asked.

"More than somewhat. It's … shall we say … pretty much no-holds-barred."

"So it isn't one of your Ben Pecos mysteries?"

Slater shook her head. "No, I try to keep those pretty much PG-rated." She looked around at her audience, inviting questions, and there were many.

Sam listened with interest as the author easily jumped between subjects as diverse as her experiences while working with the residents of Jemez Pueblo, to her upbringing in small-town Kansas, and then somewhat wild years in the heyday of San Francisco's hippie era. Sam could tell that her heart truly did resonate with the time she'd spent on her writing craft and how to sensitively portray Indian culture, which she'd studied with New Mexico's most famous writer, Tony Hillerman. Giving credit where credit was due, Susan praised Hillerman's knowledge and advice.

When a pause came in the Q&A session, Ivan piped up. "Do not forget the fabulous chocolate and signature coffee blend from Sweet's Sweets. Help yourselves and continue to enjoy book discussing."

As the members swarmed the dessert table, Ivan stepped over to Sam. "Miss Samantha, I must introduce you." He signaled to Susan Slater and beckoned the author over.

The actual introduction was superfluous. Sam knew the work of the author well, and it seemed Ms. Slater had already been briefed that Sam was the one who'd supplied the truffle cakes.

"These are completely, completely amazing!" she told Sam. "I'll be in Taos for a few days and I *will* get over to your place to see what else you have."

"Absolutely. My crew would love to meet you. Jen and Becky are both big readers. Julio … well, he's more into Harleys and tattoos."

Slater sent a big smile toward her, along with a side-eye wink. "Sounds like my kind of guy."

Sam briefly wondered whether the fact that Julio was surely at least thirty years younger would matter. The topic veered when the author told Sam she was considering moving to Taos, was actually here looking at properties. Her enthusiasm for a seemingly endless number of topics—from Southwest literature, to specialty dog breeds, to raising orchids, to coffees and pastries—drew Sam in, and she felt an instant connection.

Before the gathering broke up, they had exchanged contact information and promised to keep in touch.

Chapter 2

The Morton Library was quiet as Emily Plankhurst set aside one box of her grandfather's papers and picked up another. She'd drawn her honey-blonde hair up into a messy bun to keep it out of her eyes, and now she sat with her long legs crossed and pulled out a packet of letters to look through.

Elegant, old-fashioned handwriting crossed the envelope, showing that the sender was someone named Violet Black and the recipient was a Margaret Monroe. Emily reached for the handwritten log her grandfather had started well before she was born, and definitely prior to the digital age.

Before David Plankhurst's mind was decimated by Alzheimer's, he'd begun the practice of logging the names he encountered in his research, whether the person was known in history or not. Most were not. Still, he found interesting connections all the time, and his ultimate goal had been to catalogue the various historical materials and cross-reference names and places to make the Morton Library an authoritative place to go for New Mexico historians.

But David was unable to work now, and Grandma Valerie had predeceased him. It was Valerie who left the collection to Emily because this was the granddaughter, among any in the family, with an avid curiosity along the same lines. When Emily learned that the library could support her—largely through donations of generous patrons to keep the doors open—it took no convincing at all for her to abandon Albuquerque and move to Taos, where she could live in her grandparents' old adobe home and make the adjacent library her life's work.

She scanned the letter in her hands, adding a couple more names to the log, then refolded it and picked up the next one. Originally, she'd invited Kelly to join her for homemade stir-fry and an afternoon of the research, and she'd been somewhat disappointed when Kel cancelled. But, truthfully, the two of them would have ended up chatting away the evening and drinking a glass or two of wine, and the actual research would not have moved along as quickly with her assistance.

An hour later, the bundle of letters was logged and she filed them in the archive cabinet she'd started, trying to make better sense of the so-called system Grandfather had, which was to say, piling everything in boxes with cryptically marked labels on them. One day, she would get all the references on computer and the materials neatly catalogued. She stretched her aching back and stiff limbs and peered into the box. A couple of really old, leatherbound books—journals, most likely—were all that remained.

"Yay, almost finished a whole box," she said to the empty room.

With longing thoughts of a cup of tea and cozy pajamas, she picked up the two journals and carried them with her, locking the library before crossing the patio space to her residence. Twenty minutes later, she'd curled up in bed. She took a sip of chamomile and opened to the flyleaf of the first book.

Property of William P. Plankhurst

Emily set her mug on her nightstand and peered more closely. She was familiar with the name. William Plankhurst was her great-grandfather, Grandpa David's father. She supposed, when she thought about it, his time would have fit with the other letters from the same box. "Interesting …" she murmured as she settled into her pillows to read.

I undertake to write this account because certain unsettling events have occurred and if not for setting them to paper, I feel they may begin to dim from memory. Or I may possibly lose my mind.

Emily's heartbeat picked up a little. Seriously? What could possibly have made a no-nonsense man—as all the Plankhursts tended to be—question his own sanity?

A story has come to my attention, a tale familiar to longtime Taoseños, but one that is new to me. The tale is told of a young man who died near the very home where I live, murdered at the hand of another, by a killer who has never been caught. Most certainly, such tales exist in every town and especially during the somewhat wild days of recent years. The Old West is not quite tame, not yet, in this part of the nation, and the newer laws of Prohibition have spurred further lawlessness, with the increase in gambling halls, speakeasies, and general disregard for rules and conventions.

And why do I mention these events, although in passing? Because a scant few blocks from here is Bent Street. So named because of the home of former territorial Governor Charles Bent, whose domicile was the scene of a murderous Indian attack during the uprising. Bent Street is well known as a place frequented by ghosts—although I have not witnessed this myself, the tales are told. And not merely human ghosts. The ghostly figures of horses and soldiers are often seen there in the nighttime hours.

Ghosts and ghost horses? Emily snuggled further into the bedcovers. She actually could believe the part about ghosts. She'd had contact with the spirit of her own grandmother, Valerie, right here in this house. But ghost horses? This was the first she'd heard of that, and right on Bent Street, no more than a five or six minute walk from here. She read on.

Back to the death of the young man and his unsolved murder. I have heard the voice of someone speaking to me at times when I have worked in the library at night, and I swear to God Almighty that I believe the voice to be that of this man. He wants to tell me something important. He wants the murderer brought to justice. How can I do that? It is the question that haunts my sleep.

Emily's eyes fluttered, closing.

"I should check this out myself," she murmured.

Minutes later she was on Bent Street, the September air chilly against her skin, and she realized she'd stepped outside wearing only her pajamas and slippers.

Chapter 3

An uncharacteristic mist swirled over the sidewalk. A part of Emily's brain told her that in September the weather would be clear and crisp. Looking up, she saw stars, billions of them, and realized there were no electric lights to interfere with the beauty of the night sky. Feeling her way carefully, to avoid stepping off the curb, she puzzled over this.

Behind her would be the parking lot for the Plaza shops, but when she turned, she couldn't see it in the dark. Ahead was Bent Street, narrower by night, somehow, than in the daytime. In the distance, a church bell chimed: Two bells. A gas streetlamp illuminated the corner where Bent joined Paseo del Pueblo Norte.

"Okay, I must have dozed off longer than I thought," she murmured. *Could I have sleepwalked to get here?*

She walked toward the Governor Bent Museum, the home where New Mexico's territorial governor had been murdered during the Pueblo uprising. She'd read the stories but had not yet taken the time to tour the tiny museum since moving to town. Logic told her it wouldn't be open in the middle of the night, but the entry in her great-grandfather's diary felt fresh in her mind.

Footsteps and voices intruded, coming from behind her. She spun around.

A prickle of goosebumps rose on her arms.

Two horses, ridden by soldiers, clopped down the narrow street, hazy images. None of them turned a head in her direction, as they trotted on by. She caught only two words: Garrison Commander. Before she could form the thought that there was no garrison, no soldiers, in modern-day Taos, a human form stepped out in front of her.

She gasped and felt her heart race. Every hair rose.

"Miss?"

Emily took two steps backward.

"Don't be afraid, ma'am. I won't hurt you." The speaker's image became clearer. It was a young man, early twenties she would guess, wearing a long duster over a cotton shirt that was open at the neck, denim pants, and sturdy boots with spurs. His longish brown hair touched the shirt collar, and his beard seemed to have been recently trimmed.

"Who are you?" she asked, ready to bolt if he advanced on her.

"My name was Gabriel, Gabriel Graystone."

Wait—what? "*Was?*"

"Please don't be scared. Gabriel—I mean, *I* am—searching ..." His voice trailed off.

Emily realized that either the mist was swirling around him more intensely than everywhere else, or … his body seemed somewhat transparent. She remembered her great-grandfather's words.

"Are you really a ghost?" Seriously? Was she actually talking to some guy from the spirit world?

"I suppose so," he said, a sad tinge to his voice. "I've wandered this street, this little part of town, for more than a hundred years, and you're the second person who has spoken to me."

"Really?"

"I have experienced a few encounters, but the moment I make a sound the others have run away from me."

Emily suppressed a giggle. "Okay … Your name is Gabriel and you have nothing better to do than wander the streets at night, and you're surprised when people run away. This is just, like, too much."

His expression relaxed, and she realized he was quite handsome, with warm brown eyes and straight teeth. "When you phrase it that way," he said, "I suppose I cannot be surprised at their reactions. Too much of what?"

"It's an expression. I guess it means too much to comprehend." She glanced around and saw no one else nearby. "So, you said you were searching. Searching for what?"

His eyes grew sad. "My killer."

"Okay, whoa, wait a minute. I'm still struggling with the idea that you're a ghost … now you tell me you were murdered." The pieces clicked into place. The voice from the diary! He was still talking and she had to focus.

"That's correct. Right here on Bent Street."

"And when—"

"I believe it's been about a hundred years now, in 1920."

"Don't you think your killer is probably long gone by now?"

"Most likely, yes. But I would like to have that person identified and the historical record corrected."

Emily experienced a quick flash of the piles of boxes and drawers full of old documents in the library. Her interest quickened. Had Gabriel somehow singled out the Plankhurst family, among all the Taos residents of the past hundred years? Had he somehow known that she might be the one to answer his questions?

"Do you know who I am?" she asked, hesitating.

He shook his head. "I've not had the pleasure of an introduction."

"Um, yeah, sorry. Emily Plankhurst, librarian." She held out her hand, but he appeared not to notice.

"Emily Plankhurst." He gave a slight, very old-fashioned bow. "My pleasure."

She became aware that she was standing in front of a strange man, on a public street, in her pajamas. Now what? Gabriel's eyes were firmly fixed on hers, his expression forthright.

"So, Miss Emily Plankhurst, I apologize for being presumptuous, but I feel somewhat desperate, as you are the first person to converse with me in a very long—yes, well—may I just state it outright? Can you help me?"

"Help you find a killer who committed a murder a hundred years ago." She felt the giggles start to rise again and tamped back the urge. "Sure, yeah. Historians run in my family, and you wouldn't believe the tons of material I have. I'll give it a shot."

"A shot?"

"Bad choice of word. I mean … were you? Shot? Like, with a gun?"

He actually smiled, and it was as warm an expression as she'd imagined. "No. A knife wound. I never saw the attacker—or at least I don't remember anything of the experience. That isn't much information, is it? But thank you, Miss Emily."

"So, how do we do this? I look up information and if I find something … How will I let you know?"

"I can find you," he said. Two seconds later, he vanished into the mist.

Chapter 4

The scent of freshly baked cinnamon rolls filled the air as Sam handed off a tray to Jen, who carefully placed them in the display case. Kelly sipped on her morning coffee at one of the bistro tables, the steam rising from the cup and mingling with the sweet smell of pastries. The bell above the bakery door jingled, and Emily Plankhurst stepped inside.

"Hey, Em," Kelly said, standing to give her friend a hug. "I was planning to stop by your place in a little while."

"Morning, everyone," Emily said, her honey-blonde hair pulled back into a neat ponytail, her blue eyes wide. She had a rolled-up parchment in one hand and an old, leather-bound journal in the other. "Sam, Kelly, I had the weirdest experience last night."

"Emily, what's up?" Sam asked, her face concerned, as

she wiped her hands on a flour-covered apron.

"Please, come sit down," Kelly offered, gesturing to an empty chair where the sunlight streamed through, casting a warm glow on the old floor. As they settled around the table, Emily took a deep breath.

"Have you ever had a lucid dream? I mean one so real you would swear you actually lived the experience?"

Kelly waggled her hand back and forth a little. "I guess."

Sam said yes, definitely.

"So, last night I fell asleep reading one of my great-grandfather's old journals in which he mentioned an unsolved murder case, here in Taos."

"And you fell asleep and dreamed about it," Sam guessed.

"Kinda more than that. I met the ghost of the dead guy, and he begged me to find the killer and bring them to justice. Only thing is, it happened a hundred years ago."

"So, there would be no witnesses and no killer still around today," Kelly said.

"I know, right? And I said that to Gabriel."

"Okay, wait. You had an actual conversation with this ghost?"

"Um, yeah. I know. It sounds bizarre in the light of day, doesn't it? I woke up this morning and just laughed at myself for even coming up with such a fantasy dream. But then …" she said, opening the journal to a page marked with a ribbon, "… this is my grandfather's account of the unsolved murder case."

Kelly's green eyes widened, curiosity piqued, as she leaned in closer to examine the old book.

"This is the guy—the one I met. His name was Gabriel Graystone," Emily continued, her fingers tracing the faded ink on the journal page. "The journal agrees with everything he told me. He was killed a hundred years ago, and his murderer was never caught. But that's not the strangest part," she hesitated for a moment, unsure if she should share her next revelation.

"There's more?" Sam encouraged gently.

"In the dream, I was walking along Bent Street, just as it was back then," Emily held up the rolled parchment, which was a map. "This shows how everything was at the time." Her voice grew more animated as she described the scene, including the ghostly horses and soldiers.

"Emily, are you *sure* about this?" Kelly asked, exchanging a glance with her mother. "I mean, it was just a dream, right?"

"Normally, I'd agree with you, but this felt different," Emily insisted, her blue eyes pleading for understanding. "It was so real, and when I woke up, I knew I had to do something."

Sam's brow knit. "I've heard the tales of ghost horses and soldiers on Bent Street. That's a Taos legend that goes way back, supposedly to the time of the Pueblo Revolt when the Indians attacked in an attempt to run out the Spanish territorial government. You aren't the first to say they've witnessed that."

"So maybe I don't sound like quite such a nutcase," Emily said. "I'd love it if you two could help me put the story together."

"Sure. Let's take a look at the evidence you've gathered so far," Sam suggested. "We'll see what we can find."

"Thank you," Emily whispered, relief washing over her face as she passed the journal across the table.

Emily's fingers tapped nervously on the tabletop,

her gaze shifting between Sam and Kelly. "I know it sounds crazy," she admitted, taking a deep breath before continuing. "But I feel so certain that Gabriel's ghost is reaching out to me for help. He specifically asked for that. I … I think he wants closure."

Sam processed Emily's words. Kelly's eyes narrowed with skepticism. Behind the sales counter, Jen seemed suddenly busy rearranging the muffins. The ticking of the bakery's wall clock seemed to grow louder in the silence that followed.

"Emily," Sam began slowly, her voice tinged with concern, "it's not that we don't believe you, but … even if Gabriel's ghost is real, this is old history. Everyone he knew is surely dead now."

"Besides," Kelly chimed in, her tone cautious, "we're not really detectives. What can we discover now that the law couldn't do back then?"

Emily bit her lip, searching for the right words. "I know your doubts are reasonable, but something is telling me to see this through. You've solved mysteries before. Maybe … maybe together we could find the truth."

Sam and Kelly exchanged glances, amazed by Emily's determination. They did have their special artifacts, which had assisted them in solving crimes before, but this case felt different--older, more enigmatic.

"Please? Justice shouldn't have an expiration date," Emily continued. "We can't change the past, but we can bring closure to Gabriel and maybe to his family."

Sam sighed, unable to ignore the sincerity in Emily's eyes. "All right," she relented, placing a reassuring hand on Emily's shoulder. "We'll help you look into the case, but no promises. This is a long shot, Emily."

"Thank you," Emily breathed, her shoulders relaxing. "I know this won't be easy, but I believe we can find the answers Gabriel's been waiting for."

"So … first …" Kelly interjected, interest sparking in her eyes. "We need to figure out where to start."

Chapter 5

Sam drove the five miles home to the ranch, pleased that the days were still long enough to enjoy the fall foliage after a long day's work. The cottonwoods in town were just beginning to turn, while up on the mountainside she could see patches of aspen already in their full golden glory. She steered through the stone entry to their driveway and pulled in beside Beau's pickup truck. Both dogs raced to greet her.

"Ranger! Nellie!" Beau called out.

But the black Lab and border collie were too wound up to listen. Sam reminded herself she should dig out the recipe for her homemade dog treats and bake up a batch.

"Hey, you" Beau said, walking over to see if she needed anything carried from her truck. "Long day?"

"Mainly, I've been going over my fall recipes. Time to

start putting fresh green chile into the savories and more pumpkin into the sweets." She picked up her bag and recipe box, and they walked into the log ranch house. "I did have an interesting visit from Emily, the young librarian. You've met her."

"Yeah. Anything new in her life?"

Where to start? Beau wasn't exactly a believer in phantoms and such. "A question came up that you might know," she said. "Any unsolved murder is considered an open case, right?"

"Generally, yes. I mean, within reason."

"Hm, yeah. This one would be about a hundred years ago."

He took her jacket and hung it on the rack near the front door. "A hundred years—not likely. There does come a point when there are no more witnesses, evidence gets misplaced or damaged, and it's just not practical to call a case active anymore."

"I was afraid you'd say that."

"You could check with Evan. It's been a few years since I was there. I wouldn't even know where to start looking for the files on anything that old."

"I may do that. It could be helpful to know if the records even exist." Sam went into the kitchen and he followed. "I was thinking of warming up the green chile stew I made yesterday. Sound good?"

Beau okayed the suggestion by opening the fridge and pulling out the container while Sam located her favorite saucepan. She opened a fresh package of flour tortillas and wrapped them in foil to warm in the oven.

Fifteen minutes later they were at the dining table, and Beau brought up the subject of crime records again. "Back in my day, old documents got sent to the county building. The basement there was either a detective's dream or his worst nightmare, depending on how much he liked digging through history."

"Well, I can say for sure that Emily loves digging through old letters and documents. Could be she'd be in heaven there."

"Just run it past Evan first. You'll need authorization and contacts to go poking around." He ripped a tortilla in half and spread butter on it. "So, you said this is a murder case—any familiar names?"

"The victim was a Gabriel Graystone. Emily found an entry in her great-grandfather's diary and it sounded as if he really felt there was some kind of cover-up."

"Could have been. The 1920s were still a fairly wild time, and New Mexico was kind of at the edge of it. Statehood happened less than a decade before, and the switch from territorial government to what we have today happened in fits and starts."

"From things Emily has told me in the past, there were plenty who still treated this area as the untamed, wild west, while others were making power plays and land grabs to see who would come out on top."

He spooned up the last of his chile stew. "Wouldn't surprise me. Could turn out that your murder case was anything from a shootout on the street to an accident that got misclassified in the records."

Sam didn't mention Emily's vivid dream and how the conversation with the ghost went directly along the same lines as the diary entry from William Plankhurst. Beau's interest in the supernatural went about as far as you'd expect from a no-nonsense retired lawman and rancher.

She and the girls would be on their own to dig into this particular case.

"How about mint chip ice cream for dessert?" she asked, giving him a wink as she cleared the dishes.

Chapter 6

Emily woke the following morning before dawn, thankful for a dreamless night. She'd finished skimming through the two journals but found no other references to the Graystone family name. The old map of Taos had some strange markings, like trails of some kind, and she planned to study that a bit further today. Meanwhile, she padded to the kitchen in search of her first cup of coffee of the day.

Her reflection stared back at her as the coffee maker sputtered to life. Her hair was in tangles. She pulled it up into a high ponytail and rubbed her hands over her face to bring a little life to her complexion. She couldn't stop thinking about Gabriel and the vividness of the encounter. Of all the historical figures she'd read about in her studies, not one had come to life for her in the same way. She shook her head.

"There are no ghosts." No, scratch that. She knew of one, her own grandmother, Valerie. "Okay, there are no strange ghost men who chance to encounter a girl on the street."

At least Kelly and Sam hadn't laughed her out of the bakery yesterday. She must have come across as slightly unhinged.

Shaking her head at her own silliness, she reached for her favorite mug and poured the strong Ruta Maya coffee. After adding a generous dollop of cream, she carried the mug and meandered the rooms of her comfortable adobe home, hoping her friends hadn't changed their minds about helping her.

She loved this home—had loved it her whole life, when she came here to stay the summers with her grandparents. Worn leather couches with hand-woven blankets made by Grandma Valerie, Oriental rugs worn soft with time, shelves and niches filled with the memorabilia of a lifetime, including a couple of Maria Martinez pots. And the library. So much material yet to go through. Would she find answers about Gabriel's situation, and would she ever see him and be able to convey what she found?

By seven o'clock she was fully awake and no closer to answers. She showered quickly and dressed in soft sweats and a favorite black pullover, hair in a ponytail again, and minimal makeup, giving the day over to research and nothing else.

She was brewing a cup of tea when she heard a tap at the kitchen window.

"Kelly! I didn't realize you were stopping by."

"Neither did I. Scott insisted on taking Ana for the day.

He's such a great dad, wanting all the time he can get with her before he heads out on his book tour. So—yay me! I get a day away to do anything I want. He's thinking I'll go for a mani-pedi and then take in a movie, but I couldn't resist following through on what we were talking about yesterday. Um, if you want me to?"

"Of course! Yes, come in. Tea?"

Kelly held up a distinctive purple box from Sweet's Sweets. "These are a little rich for breakfast … and I had planned on dropping them by yesterday but time got away from me. So, maybe this can be our little reward for progress made by the end of the day. Chocolate truffle cakes."

"You are the friend of my dreams," Emily teased.

"I talked with Mom, and she says she'll try to break away from the bakery at some point this morning and can lend a hand, as well."

"Excellent." Emily grabbed two clean mugs and poured boiling water from the kettle. She pointed Kelly toward a chair and excused herself for a moment.

The morning sun cast a warm golden light over the cluttered wooden breakfast table when Emily set down her box full of evidence. Kelly leaned forward, her eyes scanning the handwritten journal entries, yellowed letters, and faded photographs that formed a window into the past.

"All right," Kelly said, rolling up her sleeves as she picked up an old letter. "Let's see what we have here."

"Most of these came from boxes on my great-grandfather's shelves," Emily explained, blue eyes flickering with excitement. "He was a historian in Taos back in the 1920s, and he kept detailed records of everything he learned about the town."

"Here's an entry about Gabriel Graystone," Kelly said, pointing to an article clipped from a yellowed newspaper. "It says he was from a prominent family in town, but his life was cut short by a tragic murder. His body was found on Bent Street, stabbed with a knife."

"Exactly what Gabriel told me," Emily replied, her voice tight. "And according to both his ghost and my great-grandfather William's notes, no one ever discovered who was responsible."

"Did your grandfather have any suspects?" Kelly asked, her green eyes narrowing thoughtfully.

"Maybe," Emily admitted, rifling through a journal. "After the entry I read the other night, I kept searching. There are some references to the Maldonado brothers, Augustine and Antonio. They were local businessmen, and William says the rumor was that they held a grudge against Gabriel for refusing to marry their sister, Clara. Something about wanting revenge for the shame they felt he brought upon their family."

"Interesting, but if they were so keen on revenge, weren't they the main suspects at the time?"

"Good question," Emily agreed. "I haven't found anything to suggest that—yet. Perhaps the sheriff and his department were too overwhelmed or didn't have enough evidence to pursue the case further."

The conversation was interrupted by another tap at the back door, and Emily got up to let Sam inside. She held out a bakery bag, which contained a half-dozen scones.

"Ooh, my favorites!" Emily raved. She got out the butter dish and three plates, filling Sam in on what they'd just been discussing.

"You're right," Sam told the girls. "Law enforcement back then was entirely up to the sheriff. Taos didn't have an official police department until much later."

"Speaking of which," Kelly continued, "I wonder if Sheriff Richardson has any old reports on the case. It's a long shot, but maybe there's something we can learn from them."

"Beau suggested that. Let me give him a call," Sam said, pulling out her phone and dialing the sheriff's direct line.

"Hey Evan, it's Sam Sweet," she greeted, putting her phone on speaker.

"Everything okay, Sam?" Evan's voice seemed neutral.

Beau's successor had been a deputy, fairly new with the department at the time of Beau's retirement, and Sam always had mixed feelings when she saw him sitting in Beau's old office. But Evan was now married to a good friend, Riki Davis-Jones, who owned Puppy Chic, the pet salon next to Sweet's Sweets. The couple were friends on a social level with all of Sam's inner circle. She reassured him that nothing was wrong at home, everyone healthy and well.

"Listen, I'm helping to look into an old murder case, and we were wondering if you had any records or reports from around 1920? Gabriel Graystone is the victim's name."

"Gosh, Sam, you're not asking much," he said with a laugh. "Actually, I understand the oldest of the crime records from the department were archived at the county building. But—that was in the old building. When they moved everything into the new one a few years ago, I have no idea what happened. I have to say, I've seen some cold cases, but nothing at all *that* old."

Sam's face fell slightly. "I'm not surprised, actually. Beau said as much. I wonder … if it turns out we need to get into those old archives, would you mind calling out there and letting the powers that be know that I might be making an inquiry? We'd really appreciate it."

"No problem. I'll do it right now, before I forget."

"Nothing he can get his hands on?" Kelly mused as Sam ended the call.

"Unfortunately, no," Sam confirmed with a sigh.

"Figures," Emily muttered, disappointment flickering in her eyes. "But we won't let this slow us down. We'll just have to get creative."

"Right," Sam agreed. "We've got plenty of other leads to follow. It's probably best to approach the county archives with some specific questions in mind, rather than showing up and expecting them to dig through it all. Let's start with these journal entries and see what else we can uncover about Gabriel Graystone's life and keep an eye out for names of witnesses or suspects."

"Good idea," Emily said.

Sam rubbed her hands together, enjoying the feel of the old paper beneath her fingertips. "Okay, so we don't have any law enforcement records. But we've got these letters, and that's something," she said, nodding toward the stack of yellowed papers on the table.

"True," Kelly agreed, pushing a lock of hair behind her ear as she scanned the faded ink. "Let's see what we can find that connects to Gabriel."

"Sounds like a plan." Emily's eyes narrowed as an idea dawned on her. "We should also look more closely into the Maldonado brothers—Augustine and Antonio. According to William's journal, and reading between the lines in this article, I'd say they had a motive and it sounds like that family was known for their ruthless ways back in the day."

She paused, her gaze flickering between her two friends. "You think they might still have descendants here in town? People who might know something?"

"Could be," Kelly mused, tapping her finger thoughtfully against her chin. "It's worth a shot, at least." She pulled out her phone and did a search. "Well, there are only a couple of Maldonados presently listed in the Taos area. We'd better dig a little, try to figure out who could be direct descendants, before we just start calling numbers."

"True." Sam gathered up the scattered letters, placing them neatly in a folder. "Em, I think you told us your grandfather had catalogued some of his materials and cross-referenced names?"

Emily nodded. "That might be the quickest way to get those names we'll need. I'm on it. That's something I can search through in the evening."

Sam spoke up again. "Tomorrow night, I'd like for Emily to take us to Bent Street, where the murder took place. There surely won't be any actual clues now, but you could show us where you were standing when you talked to Gabriel, maybe help us put everything in context. From there, we can branch out and follow any names and leads we come across."

"Sounds like a plan," Emily echoed, a determined gleam in her eye.

The day had completely slipped away, and Kelly announced she needed to get home. Long shadows filled the room; the three women stood facing one another.

"Are you ready for this?" Sam asked the question as much for herself as for the girls. "Can you believe we're seeking justice for a hundred-year-old ghost?"

"I'm excited. We can do it," Kelly replied without hesitation, her eyes meeting Sam's.

"Definitely," Emily added, her voice soft but firm. "This town is hiding a dark past and it's time to reveal that."

Chapter 7

Sam pulled two ten-inch round pumpkin-spice cake layers from the walk-in fridge and carried them to her worktable. Yesterday's research and conversation with Emily and Kelly had been exhilarating and fun, but now she wondered where they would go from there. How could they possibly track down and solve a murder case this long after the fact?

She found the tub of special buttercream frosting she'd made yesterday and set the first layer in place, coating it with the icing in a few deft strokes.

"Whatcha got there?" The voice startled her and she nearly dropped the second layer.

"Zoë! I didn't even hear you come in." Sam carefully placed the second layer, then wiped her hands and turned to hug her best friend.

"I'm in the midst of my annual, autumn deep cleaning and decided we'd better have some treats to get us through the day." Zoë rolled her eyes and straightened her loose tunic top. "I figure a good burst of sugar will keep my helpers moving. Jen's boxing up cinnamon rolls and an assortment of cookies for the crew."

"So, in answer to your question," Sam said, pointing toward the cake on the table, "we have an octogenarian birthday party with twenty-five guests. I hope everyone loves pumpkin because that's the birthday girl's favorite. I'm doing cinnamon buttercream, and the decorations will be fondant leaves and chrysanthemums. What do you think?"

"I think you're amazing to come up with so many creative ideas." Zoë laughed and scooped up a dab of the frosting that had dropped on the tabletop. "Wow—so good!"

"And if you're in the midst of deep-cleaning, I'm guessing the B&B has no guests for a few days?" Sam turned back to the cake and finished rough-coating it.

"Right. Five days until the next group arrives and we're making the most of it. Darryl's got his construction crew hopping. We're replacing windows on the north side of the place with new thermal-pane ones and painting all of the guest rooms. And I've got every one of my spare helpers busy cleaning the common areas—the parlor really needs going over—and the kitchen is practically ripped apart for a good degreasing."

"I thought you just did that."

"With that big stove of mine, it's ongoing." Zoë glanced toward the curtain that divided the bakery's sales room from the kitchen, in time to see Jen approaching with two large purple boxes. "I'd better get going," she said. "But we have to catch up soon. Maybe later in the week?"

"We'll aim for that," Sam said, wondering how wrapped up she would be with this crazy ghost hunt of Emily's.

She supposed she could back away and let the younger women handle it, since most of the action seemed to consist of going through old documents, although she had to admit her curiosity was definitely piqued by Emily's description of meeting the handsome young ghost in her dream.

She'd just started rolling fondant and cutting leaf shapes of orange, red, yellow, and green when her phone chimed. She wiped powdered sugar off one hand and tapped to accept the call from Kelly.

"How's it going this morning?" Sam asked.

"I think I've almost got Scott packed for his trip. Luckily, the man isn't fussy about clothes and he's got a favorite outfit for his presentations. He calls it his 'successful author getup.' Seriously. Brown cords, a tan shirt, and a corduroy jacket—reminds me of his professorial days at UNM. I just had to make sure he had several sets laundered and ready to go."

"He'll be gone two weeks, you said?"

"Yep, like a rock star, a different city each day."

"Wow, sounds kind of grueling."

"His publisher has booked flights, hotels, a local contact person in each place—everything. All I have to do is get him to the Albuquerque airport by six o'clock tonight."

"So, you're leaving me to go with Emily and face her ghost-guy alone, huh?"

"Looks that way." Kelly laughed. "I'm sure you can handle it."

"What about Ana? Want me to take her while you're gone?"

"Oh, no, that's no problem. She wouldn't miss seeing her daddy off at the airport, not for anything. And she's super excited that she and I will be staying in a hotel tonight. She actually wanted to go along with Scott on the book tour, and the hotel stay was the only way I could redirect her energy. We're staying at one with an indoor pool and water slide."

"That should keep her happy. So you'll be back in Taos tomorrow?"

"Yep, ready and eager to help Em some more."

Sam heard a shriek in the background and pictured five-year-old Anastasia at peak excitement. They ended the call with Sam's admonition to be careful on the highway. She finished the autumn leaves cake and boxed it for the customer to pick up, then began work on sugar-paste flowers for a wedding cake later in the week.

The everyday bustle of the bakery continued around her, with Julio making batches of muffins, scones, and cookies while Becky Gurule, her head decorator, finished two more birthday cakes and one for a quinceañera. When Sam's phone chimed this time, she saw Emily Plankhurst was the caller.

"Ready for the big adventure tonight?" Em said, practically before Sam could take a breath.

Chapter 8

It was past nine p.m. when Sam pulled her pickup truck into the public parking lot behind the Bent Street shops and shut off the engine. Only four other vehicles sat there—one she recognized as Emily's Jeep Wrangler.

"I hope I didn't mess up your evening plans with Beau," Emily said as she locked the Jeep.

"No, I'd briefed him in advance about our plans, so I just worked a bit later, placed a supply order, did some other little chores."

Emily looked around the lot. "It's not misty, like the other night. I wonder if that makes a difference."

"Em, the other night was a dream, remember?"

The younger woman blushed and laughed at herself. "See how real it felt? I seriously was not thinking that just now. Okay, reality check. I will get my head back in the present moment."

"That's fine. We're dealing with history here, so it's good that you can see our surroundings in that light. You wanted to visit the scene of the crime?"

"Right. Gabriel showed me where it happened." She led the way from the parking lot, through a passageway between shops, and onto Bent Street.

One restaurant, Lambert's, was still open, the lights cheery and a couple of cars parked out front. Otherwise, most of the shops had closed for the night. As they walked past the popular eatery, three people came out and got into one of the cars. Behind them, an employee turned the sign over to say Closed.

As the women walked down the sidewalk on the south side of the street, Emily glanced all around.

"It's much lighter tonight. I remember noting that only one street light existed then, an old-fashioned gas lamp. And the street is wider."

"I imagine it used to be only big enough for horse drawn carts," Sam said. "In the 1920s motor cars were very new, and probably scarce around here. Modern life must have forced widening a lot of the lanes in this little town, along with the addition of sidewalks."

Em pointed to an ancient cottonwood where the sidewalk veered in a curve to allow the old tree to keep its place. "That's the spot. Gabriel said he'd just walked past this tree when he was stabbed. He never saw them and can't seem to recall any details about what happened."

"It was traumatic," Sam said. "His mind could have blocked it all out."

They paused and looked around. In today's world, the north sidewalk was lined by a group of small shops.

A light was on in the one that featured art supplies, even though the place was clearly not open for business this late. The kitchen shop's display window had soft lighting and showed off a set of high-end cookware.

"I don't remember any of these from my dream," Emily said. "The buildings were here, I'm pretty sure, but they weren't the same. Of course, the mist and darkness could have hidden a lot from my view."

"And I get the feeling your eyes were on the face of a very handsome young man," Sam teased.

"Yeah, well. That too."

Sam turned and faced the west end of the street, where even the present-day width narrowed to barely a track. "Is that the direction he came from?"

"First, there were the soldiers—two of them on horseback."

"So amazing that you actually *saw* them."

Emily's eyes were glued to the dark alley at the end of the road. "Yes. Since I've been reading more of my great-grandfather's papers, I've come across the stories too. Apparently, Taos has more than one resident ghost."

"Did you come across the accounts of ghosts that hang out near *descansos*?"

"Those little crosses and memorials beside the roads? Yes! I found a video online. One lady who was interviewed said she would never, *ever* stop and pick up anyone beside the road if they were near one of those. She'd seen a man like that once and said his face was the scariest thing she'd ever witnessed."

Sam felt a shiver caress her arms. "Good thing your ghostly man wasn't like that."

"I wonder if I'll ever see Gabriel again." Em's voice

sounded wistful. Sam turned to see if she was okay, and Emily chuckled. "I'll tell you, if I do see him, I'll have a lot more questions the next time."

They had strolled to the west end of the street, almost back to the parking lot now, when they heard footsteps behind them. A woman's voice called out, "Don't worry. It's just me, Kathy Castellanos."

They'd spun around at the sound, and now saw a sixty-ish woman with long brown hair and a pleasant smile. She carried a tote bag over her left shoulder and a set of keys in her right hand.

"I own the art supply shop," Kathy explained. "Sometimes in the late evenings, after I've closed for business, is the best time to sit alone for a while and finish a painting. I do watercolors."

"I've been in your shop," Emily said. "Are those paintings yours?"

"Mostly the butterflies and flowers—my two favorite subjects."

Sam had a thought. "We've been doing some reading about Taos legends. If you're often on this street at night, have you by chance seen the ghostly people and horses that are said to show up sometimes?"

Kathy's pleasant laugh filled the air. "I have to say no, I haven't. But there's other stuff that's equally spooky. Have you been down in the tunnels?"

Sam and Emily stared at each other. "Tunnels?"

"If you have an extra few minutes, I can show you one."

"Yes, please!" Emily sounded almost a little too eager.

Kathy signaled for them to follow her back to her shop. In less than two minutes they were inside. The artist set her things down and led the way to a storage room in the back.

"Just down these stairs," she said, opening a small door that creaked noisily on its hinges. She'd picked up a small flashlight and aimed the beam down a steep wooden staircase. "Sorry about that squeal. I never use this basement space. I'm creeped out by spiders."

Emily apparently had no such phobia. She asked if she could borrow the light, then used it to see her way down. "It's not that bad," she called back up. "There's another door here. Is that where the tunnel is?"

Kathy seemed to have lost some of her nervousness once Emily went down. "Yes, that's the one. Hold on, I have a key for the padlock."

She went to a desk and quickly found a small key in the drawer. She looked at Sam. "I'll go down there if you will."

Sam felt an instant of trepidation, as Kathy seemed equally nervous about the dark, musty space. But she sent her hostess a thumbs-up.

Kathy led the way while Emily shined the light on the stair treads. She blew a layer of dust off the padlock and, using the little brass key, opened it. It hung up for a moment, then came open and the door squeaked as she pulled it toward her.

A chill wafted out through the opening. "I wouldn't be surprised if this was used for refrigeration back in the day," Kathy said. "It's always cold like this."

She held out a hand to keep Emily back. "Don't go in there. Just look. It isn't safe."

Sam immediately saw what she meant when the space was illuminated. An assortment of boards, some as narrow as two-by-fours, acted as supports for the roof. In places, the boards were propped up on rocks on the dirt floor.

They looked as though a mouse could knock them out of place and send the whole thing crashing down in a massive cave-in.

Farther in, she could see little piles of rock and dirt, most likely knocked loose over the years. She couldn't see an end, however. Judging by the direction she thought they were facing, the tunnel led under Bent Street, quite possibly toward the Plaza itself.

"I'm amazed the town hasn't closed these off, filled it all in," Sam said.

Kathy shrugged. "This is the only one I've ever seen, and that's just because the key was here when I rented my shop. Maybe other sections have been filled in."

"Or maybe the other entrances are in better shape," Emily offered. "Um, I'm guessing there *are* other entrances. Surely?"

"People have told me that the tunnels are pretty extensive," Kathy said. "A lot of the Plaza shops connect to them. Or so they say."

Sam wondered about the bakery. Although her place, and the adjacent pet salon and bookstore, were not on the Plaza, they were only a block away. No farther than Kathy's shop, but in the opposite direction.

They stared for a few moments, then Kathy spoke. "I think I've had enough. Told you, the place is creepy."

Chapter 9

After parting from Sam, Emily couldn't sleep. Dressed in old sweats, with a cup of tea at hand, she sat at her grandfather's antique wooden desk, her mind awhirl with everything she'd seen and learned in the past couple of days. The study was dimly lit by a single table lamp, which cast eerie shadows on the walls lined with bookshelves. Surrounding her were her grandfather's diaries, maps, and favorite artwork. She reminded herself that all these remnants of his life's work now belonged to her. Her eyes flickered across the pages, her mind restless yet determined to uncover the truth about Gabriel's death.

"June 15th, 1920," Emily read aloud from one of the leather-bound diaries before her. Her voice echoed softly in the room, bouncing off the towering shelves filled with books. "Visited Graystone Manor today. Had a rather odd conversation with Gabriel about the mercantile store."

Graystone Manor? This was the first she'd seen of that name. Her curiosity piqued, Emily leaned in closer to the page, her honey-blonde hair falling over her shoulder. Now why had her great-grandfather mentioned this in his diary? She'd found nothing else—yet—to indicate he and Gabriel knew each other.

And Taos Mercantile was a local institution as a Plaza business, but Emily knew little about its history or the people behind the name.

Her thoughts jumped to another set of names.

"Augustine and Antonio Maldonado," she whispered, remembering back to the two brothers whose families had become entwined with the Graystones. She recalled seeing their names somewhere among the documents she'd read, but where? She needed to get this search organized if she ever wanted a good night's sleep again.

"Is everything all right, Emily?" came a soft voice.

Valerie, her grandmother, and the resident ghost, floated into the study. Her ethereal form, wearing a long flowered skirt and turquoise tunic, was barely visible in the dim light, but her concerned expression was unmistakable.

"Grandma Valerie," Emily greeted with a slight smile. "I've been reading great-grandfather William's diaries and found mention of the Graystones. And I came across the family name Maldonado. It seems they were connected somehow."

"Ah, yes. The Graystones and the Maldonados have quite the history in this town, although I don't really know a lot about it," Valerie replied, nodding solemnly. "My dear David was cataloging his papers and documents, and I'm fairly certain he mentioned an unsavory history between the two families. You may want to look into that further."

"Thank you, Grandma," Emily whispered. At least this was small confirmation that she might be on the right track.

She set the diary aside and went to the card drawer she'd discovered recently. The antique wooden cabinet held three-by-five index cards where David, her grandfather, had begun a system of cross-referencing names and places in the area. She flipped to the G's, but only found six cards with the Graystone name: Graystone Manor, with an address; and the surname Graystone, and first names listed below it. Charles, Amanda, Nathaniel, Richard, Silas, and Gabriel. Dates beside each name were intended to show the birth and death dates, but these were incomplete, waiting for more information. Judging by the format in which they were written, Emily assumed Charles and Amanda were the parents and the other names were Gabriel's brothers.

The remaining four cards had the name Graystone written at the top but no further notations at all. To create those cards, but leave them blank, seemed to tell her that her grandfather had somehow been preoccupied with the Graystone family, that he had much more data to enter and hadn't.

She felt a wave of frustration that her grandfather hadn't detailed the information more thoroughly. Then she brought herself up short. Alzheimer's was no trivial thing. It certainly wasn't Grandpa's fault he'd run out of time to complete his life's work. She thought of the library shelves filled with books and documents, then at the boxes of material she'd not had time to go through yet. She sighed. She might not have time to completely catalogue everything in this building in her lifetime, either.

She picked up the diary again, unable to shake the

feeling that she was on the verge of discovering something significant. As if whatever secrets lay hidden within these dusty old pages held the key to unraveling a mystery that had lingered in the shadowy streets of Taos for a century.

Valerie's soft voice spoke up again. "I know, sweetheart. Your grandfather spent many evenings doing this very thing."

Emily's backside was aching from sitting in the same position in the old chair. "Maybe I'll carry this to the living room and settle on the couch, or read in my bed." Another cup of chamomile tea sounded good.

She picked up the diary but the pages fell open and something drifted to the floor.

Emily's fingers trembled as she reached for the old, yellowed paper. Forgetting the tea and a more comfortable seat, she carefully unfolded it and began to read. The old-fashioned handwriting revealed a letter, dated 1920.

Dearest Gabriel, Emily read, her eyes skimming across the page. *I cannot understand why you refuse to marry me. Our families have been intertwined for generations, and such a union would only strengthen our bond …*

"So, it's true. Gabriel Graystone refused to marry Clara Maldonado," she murmured to herself. The implications were staggering. If they had married, the feud between the two families might not have escalated the way it did. But why did he refuse? What secret lay hidden beneath the surface of this seemingly simple love story?

"Emily, sweetheart?" Valerie's voice interrupted her thoughts. "You seem troubled."

"Listen to this," she said, sharing the contents of the letter. "Gabriel broke Clara Maldonado's heart. I feel so sad for her."

"Perhaps it broke his heart too. As for those brothers of hers, revenge can be a powerful motivator," Valerie agreed, her eyes narrowing. "But there must be more to it than that. Perhaps you should look at what was being said after your young man's death."

"He's *not* my young man," Emily asserted, blushing. "But you're right. The library has a few old newspapers in the archives. Not a complete collection, by any means, but I might find something. And at least those are filed already in the correct date sequence."

She carried the diary and letter with her and walked out to the library, to the shelves where bound copies of newspapers sat. Her great-grandfather had started this collection and had neatly lettered dates on the spines of the leather bindings. She went to the summer of 1920, when Gabriel died, and pulled out volumes pertaining to the remainder of that year and all of 1921.

Eventually, she came across a newspaper article from 1921, where the familiar names cropped up not in the news section but in the gossip pages. The anonymous writer of the column suggested that Augustine and Antonio Maldonado may have taken revenge against 'a certain contemporary of theirs who has met his demise.'

The gears turned in Emily's head as she tried to piece together the puzzle, but the skimpy clues were pretty cryptic. How much of it was rooted in the actions of two vengeful brothers?

"Grandma," Emily whispered. "Are you still here? I think we need to find out more about Augustine and Antonio Maldonado. Just tonight I learned about the tunnels under the town. I'm thinking those tunnels could reveal something important."

"Go with caution," Valerie said. "I've heard tales of the tunnels but never experienced a visit there. Those dark places are very old and could be extremely dangerous."

Feeling the lateness of the hour, Emily carefully placed the letter back into her grandfather's diary and trudged across the patio to her house. As she crawled back into her rumpled bed, she had a feeling the motivations of those two brothers would be crucial to unraveling the tangled web of deceit that had ensnared the Graystones and the Maldonados for over a century.

Chapter 10

Grammie, can I cut out the cookies today?" Ana sat at the worktable, wearing a size small baker's jacket that still needed the sleeves rolled up to fit her tiny frame. She was eyeing the ball of chilled dough Sam had carried in from the walk-in fridge.

"Are your hands clean?"

Ana stared at them for a second. "I'm pretty sure they are."

"In the bakery we need to make absolutely sure." Sam scooped her granddaughter up from the stool and carried her to the sink where she supervised the use of soap and warm water. "Okay, now I think you can cut out cookies."

"I wanna do some ghosts!"

"Well, I was thinking of these leaves. Normally we only do ghosts in October."

Ana shook her head, a stubborn pout on her mouth. "Nuh-uh, there are ghosts all the time, not just at Halloween."

Well, that was certainly true, if Emily's various experiences were real.

"You know, I think you're right. I'll find our ghost for you. Meanwhile, maybe you can do a few oak leaves to get started."

The little girl waited impatiently while Becky rolled a ball of dough to the right thickness and set it in front of her. Sam went to the bins where she kept seasonal items sorted by holiday. The ghost cookie cutter would be right there in the container with the pumpkins, witches, and (her own favorite) a big triangle she always tri-color iced as candy corn. She delivered the ghost and a pumpkin to Ana at the table.

"I think these both work for September, don't you?" she told her little helper with a smile.

Assured that Ana was in heaven, Sam turned to check the status of the day's orders. Becky had finished a wedding cake that needed to be delivered to the banquet room of a hotel this afternoon. Sam had offered to do it. She could take Ana along for that and a few errands, and then it would be time for Kelly to pick her up.

They finished the cut-out cookies, ate some of the remaining breakfast quiche for lunch, and then headed out to make their delivery.

"I love wedding cakes," Ana said, as Sam buckled her into the backseat of her Sweet's Sweets delivery van. "They're so huge!"

Today's delivery was a fairly complex order—five tiers of cream and yellow, plus a groom's cake and individual ones for certain honored guests to take home.

"When I get married, I want mine to be just like this one," Ana declared.

"Well, then, just to be sure I remember that, I'll take a picture of it right now," Sam told her with a smile, pulling out her phone.

Then, to verify, she phoned the venue to make certain someone was on hand at the hotel to accept delivery. Oh, yes—the event coordinator assured her, an entire crew was setting up and decorating for the early evening wedding.

Sam made that their first stop, and within twenty minutes all of the delicate cakes were someone else's worry.

"Shall we stop in at the B&B?"

"Yay—Auntie Zoë! I love her house—it's huge!"

Huge seemed to be the theme of the day with Ana, Sam thought with a grin. She pulled onto Kit Carson Road and headed toward the small lane where the large adobe sat among big cottonwoods and elms and where Zoë kept her spectacular gardens immaculate. Asters, mums, and lilies were in autumn bloom as they entered the service drive that led to the back door. Two pickup trucks with the name of Darryl's business sat there already, and Sam pulled to one side so they could come and go if needed.

"Here's a gift for Aunt Zoë," Sam said, handing Ana the small bakery box that contained mini-cheesecakes and some of their cutout cookies from this morning. "Do you want to carry it in?"

It was practically a rhetorical question. Of course she did.

Zoë met them at the back door and held the screen wide open. "Hey you guys. You're just in time for afternoon tea."

"Are you sure you have time for a break? We were out on a delivery and just wanted to bring some of Ana's special fall cookies by. I know you're swamped."

"This time of day I'm more than ready to be off my feet for a minute. I've already got the kettle on and my favorite teabags out." She led the way into her warm and friendly kitchen.

"Okay, then, it's a deal. Honey, put the cookies there on the big table."

The kettle began to whistle and Zoë turned the burner down low. She pulled out a few sheets of blank paper and a canister with markers and crayons, setting them on the table for Ana. Creating some fabulous piece of crayon art was one of their rituals, and Ana immediately climbed up on a chair and set to work.

Zoë poured tea, making one safer for Ana with the addition of cold water. She placed the cookies on a nice plate.

"Sam, grab your mug and come this way. I'd love your opinion on the colors we chose for the guest rooms," she said.

The two women set off down the hall where three of the five guest rooms were situated. Sam noted that the large dining room was filled with rolled-up rugs, nightstands, lamps, and accessories.

"Looks like the project has really uprooted you."

"Well, it's about the only way to get a lot done on short notice. You'll be surprised. Four of the rooms are painted already, and all the new windows are in place. Within a day or two, Darryl's crew will have all the furniture moved back, I'll put the finishing touches in place, and you'll never know this mess existed."

"Wow, amazing. You're so efficient."

"It helps to have a whole construction crew at my beck and call. And, it's not the first time we've done this." Zoë pointed the way into the first bedroom.

Although the queen-sized beds were stripped and covered in plastic drop cloths, Sam could see that the walls and trim were done. A little cleanup and the furniture could be set back in place.

"I love the earthy, warm colors," she exclaimed as Zoë walked her from one room to the next.

"I just can't get my head around the stark all-white or shades-of-gray décor that's so prevalent these days. We want our guests to experience New Mexico; terra cotta, pale turquoise, coral, and gold just fit our vibe so much better. Nothing that feels like a plain old hotel room that could be in any city in the world."

Sam agreed. Those were the colors Zoë often wore, along with purple, and her beautiful home reflected that. "Your guests will love it. I love it!"

"Good. So, what's been going on in your lives?"

"Did I mention that Kelly and I have become somewhat wrapped up in a mystery involving a ghost?"

Zoë's expression registered surprise.

"Yeah, it's Emily's deal. It's a bit unbelievable, really." She stared out a bedroom window that overlooked the garden. "Have you ever heard of tunnels that run under the town?"

"Here, in Taos?"

"Well, it's true. I was out with Emily last night—long story about the ghost guy—and a shop owner showed us one of the tunnel entrances under her art shop on Bent Street."

"Hmm, amazing."

"She told us there's supposedly a whole network of them, with entrances under many of the shops near the Plaza. The one she showed us looked pretty rickety. I'd be worried it might collapse."

Zoë stared into space. "I have to say, I learn new things about this town all the time, even though I've lived here most of my life."

"True. And that makes me wonder … Do you know anything about either a family called Graystone or some Maldonados? Both would have been here about a hundred years ago."

"Maldonado, yes. It's a fairly common name in New Mexico, although I don't recall there being many of them around here now. But Graystone … The mercantile shop on the Plaza used to bear that name. It became Taos Mercantile when it was bought by another family. I've never met them."

Sam agreed, filing away the information. A small voice interrupted her thoughts.

"Grammie, what do you think of my picture?" Ana held out her drawing.

Sam stared at the picture, a scene of a deserted street at night. And the thing that sent a chill up her arms was the fuzzy figure of a man in a long coat and cowboy hat standing near a large tree. How on earth had a five-year-old come up with this? Sam shook off the feeling. Ana must have overheard some of the recent conversations and simply put her imagination to work.

Ten minutes later, they'd said their goodbyes and were on their way back to Sweet's Sweets.

Chapter 11

The smell of old leather and parchment filled Emily's nostrils as she entered the library, only to find it in chaos. Books and papers covered every surface, some even floating in midair, caught up in a whirlwind of supernatural energy. She gasped, her vivid blue eyes scanning the dusty space for any sign of danger.

"Gabriel?" she called out, her voice barely above a whisper.

"Emily," replied Gabriel's ghost, materializing before her. His ethereal form shimmered like a mirage, his old-fashioned attire a testament to his time. "I apologize for the mess. I've been searching for something important."

"Like what? What's so important that you needed to wreck my place?" Emily's gaze flicked between him and the books, which were now settling to the floor. "What's going on?"

"Since you've learned about my connection to the Maldonado family and their possible involvement in my murder," Gabriel explained, his voice tinged with urgency, "I need you to know about the tunnels beneath our town."

"I already know. But please, tell me more," Emily asked.

"An intricate network of hidden passages runs under the very streets we walk on," Gabriel told her. "They connect various shops and homes, including this library. I drew a map of them in 1919, and I was hoping your grandfather had it." He gestured toward the scattered papers in frustration.

"Are these tunnels related to your murder or the feud?" Emily inquired, her curiosity piqued.

"Maybe both. The Maldonados used to use the passageways for something secretive. I don't know what, but the truth lies down there somewhere," Gabriel replied cryptically. "But first, we must find my map."

"All right, let's start looking," Emily agreed, "but can we do it in an orderly way?"

Kneeling on the floor, Emily combed through the disarray left by Gabriel's desperate search. She stacked books to one side and loose documents in another pile, which Gabriel began to sort through.

Her thoughts wandered to the Maldonado brothers and the role they may have played in the tragic events. Could it be that their desire for vengeance led them to commit murder? The answer must be here somewhere. Or in the tunnels. Or in public records. The size of the enormous task hit her as she stared at the mountains of uncatalogued information.

A sound at the door interrupted her thoughts, and

Gabriel faded away in an instant.

"Chicken," she teased, sending a frown toward the space where he'd been standing.

She walked over to open the door and saw one of her regular patrons standing there.

"Oh, sorry! Looks like I interrupted something, um … messy. We did have an appointment this morning, didn't we?"

"It's fine, Mr. Lighthouse. I was just sorting through some papers and, hm, I guess the time got away from me." She turned to hide the fact that she'd completely forgotten he was coming. "Do come in … let me move some of this clutter …"

The customer, a scholarly man in his seventies who was studying the history of the Santa Fe Trail, edged into the room and waited while she stacked the fallen books on the desk and then excused herself to retrieve from the back room the materials she'd located for him.

"I think these two books will be most helpful in your research," she told him, returning with a slender volume and a much thicker one. "One covers the basics and includes maps of the trail. The other has personal stories of pioneers who traveled the route. Some of their recounts are fascinating as they describe the landmarks they watched for, how they knew of places to stop for the night, and where there would be water. Many of the hardships of the trail."

"Oh, these are excellent," Lighthouse said.

"Let me just have you sign them out. There's no official due date to return them, but it's helpful to our other patrons if we keep things circulating at least every couple of weeks." She led him to the front desk where she kept track of checkouts on her computer.

"I'll dive right into them when I get home," he told her. "Shouldn't take me more than a few days to make a lot of notes."

"And there's more, plenty more," she said. "I just didn't want to overwhelm you with everything at once."

He gave a smile and picked up the books, seeming less worried by the clutter than when he'd arrived. Emily saw him out the door, then locked it as he drove away.

"Well, that was a little embarrassing," she said to the empty room. "Nobody's ever seen the place looking like a tornado hit."

"Sorry." Gabriel's ghost reappeared, looking contrite. "The good news is, I think I've found the map!"

"Did you actually remove those documents from the premises? You can't do that!" Her stomach felt as though a rock had settled there. What if he'd taken her grandfather's important work and vanished with it forever?

"I brought everything back." He held out a tattered sheet of paper bearing a detailed sketch of the town, with its web of underground passages carefully marked in ink. Emily's heart raced as she took it, hoping that this was the key to unlocking the truth.

Chapter 12

Next stop, the town archives, Emily decided. Gabriel's map was one he'd drawn from memory and nothing appeared to scale. Not to mention, none of the businesses or references points were the same today. At least with official records she should be able to find something more definitive, either to corroborate or to refute his notes.

She double-checked her appointment calendar to be sure another patron wasn't due to show up at any minute, then locked up and went out to her Jeep. Despite ongoing street construction, she was parking at the county building ten minutes later. Inside, she made her way to the records department, then to the woman she'd been told handled the historical documents.

"Tunnels under the Plaza?" The clerk was staring at her as if she'd sprouted horns.

"I know they exist—at least one does. I've seen it. I just need to know if some kind of diagram or map exists that shows the whole network of them."

"I've worked here ten years. Never heard of it."

"Is there someone who's been here longer, maybe a real old-timer?"

"Francisco Maes." The clerk leaned closer. "He was old when I started. He's ancient now."

"Does he still work here?"

A shrug. "He did, as of last week. I'll check." She walked through a doorway in one corner. Fifteen minutes passed at a snail's pace before she returned. "He's on break. You can wait if you want."

The idea of sitting around made Emily realize she hadn't eaten in hours, and the tiny carton of yogurt she'd had at six a.m. was no longer giving her any energy. "I'll come back. Can you pass along to him what I need?"

The clerk turned her back and looked at the others in the waiting area. "Next?" she called out.

Okay, not helpful. Emily suddenly had a craving for a spicy chicken sandwich from Wendy's, which was just across the street. She left her car in place and walked over.

The toot of a horn grabbed her attention as she was about to walk across the fast food place's parking lot. The familiar delivery van from Sweet's Sweets turned in and the side window powered down.

"Hey, Sam, what's up?"

"Well, I didn't get any of the promised research done yet. I had Ana all morning, we did a few errands, and I just delivered her back to her mom."

"Research?" Em's mind went blank. "Guess I'm hungry. Want to come inside with me?"

Sam parked the van and joined her. "I promise I'll get back on the search for Maldonados and Graystones this evening at home."

Emily quickly placed her order and they took seats inside the cool restaurant. "I had an interesting morning and forgot all about eating lunch. But this—" she reached into her messenger bag and pulled out a document inside a large plastic zipper bag. "This showed up in the library."

"Showed up?"

"With a little help from you-know-who." Emily eyed the clerk who'd carried her food over. Once the kid walked away, she looked Sam in the eye. "Yes, Gabriel was in the library when I walked in this morning. We searched through a lot of uncatalogued papers, and he came up with a map. Told me he drew this himself, a century ago, when he first discovered the tunnels and explored them."

Sam took the map and turned it over. "Do you think it's accurate?"

"I'm trying to find out. A little bureaucratic delay over at the county building, but I'm going back after I eat and will try to catch up with a Francisco Maes who has supposedly worked there since God was a kid."

Sam chuckled. "Could be promising."

"If this Mr. Maes can lead me to some kind of official diagram or blueprint of the tunnels, I'll feel better about believing Gabriel's version."

"And if not?"

"I know it's possible that the tunnels were completely undocumented, that they were dug for some not-quite-legal purpose like hiding runaway slaves or concealing bootleggers, or … who knows." Emily pushed her fries toward Sam, offering to share, as she took the first big bite of her sandwich.

"I get the feeling you'll want to go down there anyway, even if there are no other maps." Sam picked up one of the fries and dipped it in ketchup. "I have to say, I don't like the idea. We saw how precarious that entryway looked. The whole thing could come crashing down."

"I know. That's why I'm hoping to find someone else who's more familiar with them. It's very possible that other tunnel entrances are in much better shape than the one we saw."

"Possible, yes. Likely? Ooh, I don't know."

Emily wiped her lips with a napkin, her expression brightening. "I don't know why I didn't think of this before. Kelly and Scott introduced me to a professor from the local UNM campus, a guy who's into cave exploration. He's got gear and even some equipment that can take readings to see if an area is steady or not. I could run all this by him, see if he's aware of the tunnels."

"Maybe he's actually already explored them," Sam suggested.

"That would be good. And if not, at least he'd probably be interested in going down there with me—properly equipped, of course. We'll see what information Mr. Maes can offer."

Sam gave her the side-eye. "Just be careful. And do *not* go down there alone."

Chapter 13

By four o'clock Emily was almost ready to call the search of the county archives a total bust. Francisco Maes was a nice enough old guy, not quite as jaded as the clerk up front, but said there were no documents like she was looking for. She thanked him and turned to leave.

"I might know something, though," he said, "something that's not written down."

She took him by the elbow and suggested they take a little walk. In the parking lot, away from the ears of officialdom, he went into a story. He'd heard of the tunnel system, actually remembered a time when he was a kid and the son of the guy who owned the jewelry store (which he admitted was no longer there) showed him a secret doorway in the basement. The two boys had crept through the opening and sneaked along a dirt passageway until they came up in the root cellar of the Hotel La Fonda.

"You're sure of this? So, your friend's dad's business was next door to the La Fonda?"

"Oh, *si*, most definitely. The tunnel we were in was not long at all. We came to an opening and there were a lot of stacked boxes, potatoes and things like that. We walked out into the kitchen of the hotel and sneaked right through the dining room and out the front doors of the lobby."

"And the tunnel wasn't caved in or anything like that?"

"Oh, no. It was nice, framed with wooden braces."

"And you think there are more tunnels like that?"

A huge shrug. "My friend said so. He bragged that he used to run around all over the town that way."

"And this was how long ago?"

"Eh, almost sixty years ago maybe. We were about ten, twelve years old." He gave a crooked smile that showed a couple of missing teeth. "Fun times. Kids then were a lot more free, not watched every second by their parents, not tied down to those little screens." He mimed what every kid looked like, staring at a phone and thumbing away.

She returned his smile. "I know what you mean—well, kind of. Thank you so much for sharing your story."

He walked back into the building and she went to her car. Although there was a more direct route back to the library, she detoured into the Plaza and cruised all four sides. The shop next to the hotel was now filled with outdoor gear, but she felt certain the size and layout would be the same. Basements don't change a whole lot, she reasoned, although another owner along the way might have blocked off the tunnel entrance or built something in front of it. But she was eager to take the next step.

She drove home and walked into the library. The late

afternoon sun slanted through the high windows, casting shadows across the desk and library table. The stacks of books and papers appeared exactly as she'd left them.

"Gabriel," she called out, "it's time. I'm ready to explore the tunnels."

Chapter 14

Sam drove away from the fast food place, thinking about her promise to Emily to research the Maldonado and Graystone names. She needed to get back to the bakery at some point, to leave the delivery van and pick up her own truck. But that could wait. The sheriff's department was practically on the way.

She made her way through the road construction zone and past the Plaza entrance. At least most of the summer tourists were gone now. She parked in the department's lot and walked through the front door. Things were so similar to when Beau was sheriff, but there were subtle differences too, a new face at the front desk, the scent of coffee gone.

She told the newbie who she was and that she wanted to see Evan Richards if he was in. Rather than waving her through, as Dixie would have, the deputy on the desk called Evan forward.

"Hey, Sam," he said, giving her a hug. "What can I do for you?"

She shot a smug look—sorry, couldn't help it—at the woman running the desk, as Evan led her back through the squad room and into the private office that used to be Beau's.

"I think I already mentioned I'm looking into a murder that goes back a hundred years ..."

"Right." He took the seat behind the desk.

"Two names have come up—Graystone and Maldonado—and I wonder if there are any current day descendants I might talk to. I have to say, since the demise of the telephone directory, this is not a simple task. Social media doesn't quite fill the need."

He laughed at that. "And you're wondering if any of them might have a criminal record?"

"I did have that thought."

"I can't give out much detail, you know ..."

"Which is fine. A name and address would be great."

He pulled his keyboard forward and tapped a few keys. "I'm not showing anyone in the county named Graystone. You are aware of the old Graystone Manor, off of 68? The place is fairly derelict now. No one living there. And I don't have enough history here, to tell you where the family went or is rumored to have gone. Beau might know more."

She filed away the fact of the old house, although she couldn't see what bearing that would have if no one lived there.

"Now, Maldonado ... I'm seeing a couple of names, both at the same address. Charges go back more than five years, doesn't seem either of them are trouble makers in the present time."

She raised an eyebrow.

"Yes, I'll give you the names. It's up to you to ask the questions and see if that line of the family has been in Taos a long time." He pulled a small notepad over and jotted some names.

"John Maldonado and Eric Maldonado, brothers," Sam read. "And the address is on Salazar Road."

"Yep. Like I said, we don't have a record of any problem since the bar fight back in 2017."

"Are there other family members listed at that residence?"

"There could be more, but we only have those who got involved in the altercation at the time. They were young, barely twenty-one according to their IDs." He sent her a look that said he was well aware those might have been fake. "Exchanged words with some other young bucks, probably over a girl or two … you know how that goes."

"So, it's likely they still lived at home with their parents?"

He shrugged. "Could be."

She understood. He was sharing everything he could. Most likely the boys had appeared in court and been sentenced to some kind of community service or minimal time in county jail. If the fight hadn't included weapons or gotten anyone killed, it wouldn't have warranted a lot of attention by law enforcement. Hopefully, they were good kids who'd learned a valuable lesson. That's often how it went.

Sam glanced at her phone screen on her way out. It was a little after four. She could do her vehicle exchange and drive out to Salazar Road on her way home. Might be a good time to catch someone if they were arriving home from work and starting dinner.

Twenty minutes later, she took Salazar Road, spotted the house on the left and parked across the street, rehearsing her opening lines as she walked up the gravel pathway to a slumping adobe that could have easily been a hundred years old.

Neat flowerbeds held hollyhocks that were mostly spent, and some kind of tall plant with yellow flowers, which Sam didn't recognize. Crape myrtle, now turning red, covered the perimeter chain link fence. She approached the front door. There was no doorbell so she rapped on the frame of the screen door.

A woman about her age answered, wiping her hands on a kitchen towel, her dark eyes inquisitive.

"Hi," Sam said, introducing herself as the owner of Sweet's Sweets because that often brought some degree of recognition from locals. "I'm looking for a Maldonado family that's lived here in Taos for more than a hundred years. I'm sorry if this is a bother, but yours is the first family with that surname that I've located."

The woman stared, her expression saying, *what is it you want from me?*

"It's for a research project the library is conducting, trying to gather information on longtime Taoseños. I've been assigned to get names in the families of Maldonado and Graystone who lived here in the early 1900s, maybe 1920s."

"My husband is who you should talk to. Jaime. He'll be home in about thirty minutes. But I can tell you now, his grandmother would have been the one to ask. She grew up here, probably about that time."

"Do you suppose I could get some names? There's a lot of archived material I can look through, if I know what names are pertinent."

She glanced over her shoulder. "Look, I've got something on the stove. Come in for a minute. I'm Annette, by the way."

"Thanks, Annette. I'm really sorry to disturb your meal preparations. I'm on the way home to do the same, so I won't take long."

She followed the woman through a messy living room, into a kitchen filled with the heavenly scent of green chile and onions. A pot on the stove was bubbling like crazy and Annette rushed to give it a stir and turn down the heat.

"Now, you were asking about several names of old timers?"

"Right. Specifically, Graystone. Does that ring a bell?"

Annette shook her head. "Not really. Well, there's that old house off of 68. I think that part of town has filled in with newer homes now, but I remember that one being kind of a standout, built of gray stone instead of adobe."

"Interesting. I'd heard of it but didn't realize what kind of rock it was built of."

"Yes. Hold on. There are some old family albums that *abuelita* left behind. Jaime's grandmother lived with us the last few years of her life. She passed last year and I haven't had time to sort through a lot of her things."

Annette crossed the room and opened a rustic pine cupboard that probably had come from Mexico in its early life. She pulled out a leatherbound album and motioned for Sam to take a seat at the kitchen table. She opened the wide pages and stared at the array. "This adobe house, that's *abuelita's* little place where she raised her family. I recognize her sons—Jaime's dad and his uncles."

Sam guessed the time frame to be later than Gabriel

Graystone's era. Judging by the clothing, these were pictures taken in the 1940s. She felt disappointment.

Movement outside the window caught their attention. "Oh, there's Jaime now. Maybe he can go through the pictures with you while I finish making my enchiladas."

"It's incredibly nice of you to take the time for this," Sam said, making sure she had a smile on her face when Jaime Maldonado came walking in the back door. He wore a uniform shirt from one of the local car dealers, dark blue twill with his name embroidered on a patch on the breast. He smelled of garage oil and dust.

While Annette briefly described what this stranger was doing in their house, Sam paged a bit deeper into the album, stopping when she came to some shots that showed automobiles and clothing of the 1920s.

"Dinner will be ready in about forty-five minutes," Annette said, offering her husband a beer while he washed his hands at the kitchen sink.

"I won't take much more of your time," Sam assured them. "I noticed these pictures seem to be taken in the era we're looking at for our research, so we can just focus on them, if that's okay."

Jaime, a man of few words, took a long swig from the beer bottle and glanced at the photo she was pointing to. "My *abuela*, when she was young," he said, pointing to a sturdy-looking woman in a dress that hit mid-calf. "And *abuelo*. He was a good man."

"Do you know any of the others in the photos?" She pointed to one that included an Anglo man and two couples dressed in flapper styles.

He shook his head but reached for the picture and pulled it gently from the four little paper corner pieces that held it in place. "*Abuelita* was very good at labeling things." He turned the picture over and studied names that had been neatly penciled on the back. "I believe these are her brothers."

Sam glanced at the names. None was Antonio or Augustine. None of the women was Clara.

Jaime handed the photo to her. "Sorry, I gotta excuse myself a minute." He headed down a hallway.

Sam looked toward Annette, who was quick-frying tortillas to soften them, her back turned to Sam. She replaced the photo Jaime had removed from the album and quickly took out another. None of the names she needed appeared. Another, same result. Some of the photos clearly included friends of the family. An Iris Maxwell and a Betty Cordova appeared in several, both in their teens or early twenties, both dressed for some social occasion, by the look of their modern clothing. Sam guessed they were dates of two of the Maldonado brothers. Or they could have been neighbors. When Jaime returned, she pointed them out but he shook his head, not recognizing either.

Annette had finished assembling her chicken enchiladas and setting the baking dish in the oven, and Sam was feeling guilty for having interrupted their afternoon. She thanked them both, apologized again, and made her way out to her truck.

Chapter 15

Be careful, Emily," Gabriel warned, his ghostly face concerned. "There are secrets buried down there that some might rather not see brought to light."

"Let's just see what we find," Emily replied, clutching the map tightly, "I need your help to make my way around."

With the map in hand, Emily entered the back room at the library, the place her grandfather always used to conduct his studies. The room was dimly lit, with the sun casting golden shadows. Gabriel pointed toward the towering bookshelf that lined one wall, its shelves sagging beneath the weight of the old books.

"Gabriel, are you sure this is where the entrance is?" she asked, scanning the walls for any sign of a hidden passageway.

"Absolutely," the ghost replied, hovering behind her.

"Look for a book about the horsemen of Spain. It should be toward the bottom."

Emily squatted down, fingers running along the spines of dusty books until she found the one she was looking for. As she pulled it out, the shelf groaned and slowly swung inward, revealing a black chasm beyond.

"Ohmygosh, it actually worked," she murmured, her heart pounding in her chest as she peered into the darkness. The atmosphere felt damp, heavy with the aged scent of air that had not stirred in many years. She hesitated for a moment, observing the debris-strewn tunnel floor. At least this one wasn't propped up by rocks and boards.

"Is it safe?" she asked Gabriel, her voice wavering despite her best efforts to sound confident.

"Of course, Emily. I used to walk these tunnels myself, back when I was alive," he reassured her, his ghostly form glowing faintly in the gloom. "I'll stay with you every step of the way, I promise."

Yeah, well, that was a hundred years ago, she thought, summoning up all the bravery she could muster. She picked up the small daypack she'd prepared with a few essentials for exploring.

"All right," she sighed, taking a deep breath. Emily reached for a flashlight from her pack, switching it on and casting a beam of light into the darkness. "Here goes nothing."

As she stepped inside, the cool dampness of the tunnel walls pressed in around her. Her footsteps echoed softly through the confined space. She shivered, feeling the chill seep into her bones.

"Remember, Emily, there are people who would rather these secrets stay hidden. We must be cautious," Gabriel warned, his voice barely a whisper as they ventured deeper into the tunnel.

"Trust me, I'm well aware," Emily replied, her thoughts drifting to the Maldonado brothers and their potential involvement in Gabriel's murder. "I'm less afraid of people than of the structure itself."

"Brave words, my dear," he said, admiration evident in his tone. "You truly have the heart of a Plankhurst."

Curious. How would he know that? "Thanks, Gabriel," she smiled, feeling a little more at ease with her spectral companion by her side. "Now, let's find out what's been hidden down here for so long."

The tunnel widened slightly and they pressed on through the darkness, following the flickering circle of light from Emily's flashlight. She wanted to believe that every step carried them closer to the truth.

They came to an intersection, where a branch of the tunnel turned—she guessed—northward. Almost at once, a strong gust of wind whipped through the narrow passage. The flashlight flickered wildly as she stumbled forward, feeling suddenly disoriented. Her heart raced with a mix of fear and exhilaration as the breeze intensified, whipping her hair about her face.

"Gabriel? What's happening?" she called out, gripping the flashlight tightly in her hand.

"Stay calm, Emily. Trust the magic," he urged her, his ethereal voice barely audible.

Darkness enveloped her. She felt panicky. But then she remembered Gabriel's words—trust the magic. As quickly as it had come, the wind died down and the space became visible again. She looked around and realized the tunnel was in much better shape here, its earthen walls smooth and solid. They were facing a doorway. They stepped through it and ascended concrete steps, emerging in an alley.

"Where are we, Gabriel?" she asked, catching a slight tremble in her voice.

"Look around, Emily. The answer is right before your eyes."

She took a few steps beyond the alley and gasped. There was Taos Plaza sprawled before her, but it felt different. Vendors and townspeople milled about, dressed in old clothing. No, not old, just old-fashioned. Many were well-dressed—men in suits and cravats, women in knee-length dresses and cloche hats. Carts held a variety of fruits and vegetables, fresh bread, plucked chickens, along with leather goods, purses and belts, and silver crafts. She caught the scent of wood fires, where Indian women in long skirts were preparing fry bread.

"Is this … Have we traveled back in time?" she whispered, her eyes wide with wonder.

"I believe … we have," Gabriel replied, his ghostly form taking on a more solid appearance. "Welcome to Taos in my day."

"Unbelievable. No freaking way," she muttered, her mind reeling from the implications.

"The paranormal has a way of surprising even the most skeptical among us," he said, an amused smile playing on his lips. "Come, we have discoveries to make."

Emily adjusted the strap of her backpack and took a step forward, masking her trepidation, staying alert for clues to the secrets that had been hidden for a century.

"Gabriel, will we be able to return to our time?" she asked, her voice betraying more than a hint of anxiety.

"Have faith, Emily," he reassured her. "I'm sure we

were brought here for a reason, and the same power will guide us home when the time is right."

"Okay …" she replied, taking a deep breath to steady herself. What choice did she have? "Let's do this."

Voices and laughter filled the air as Emily stared at the Plaza, feeling like an intruder in a time where she didn't belong. Everything was familiar, yet different. Across the way was the Hotel La Fonda, very similar to the present-day version. Just ahead, where Taos Mercantile sat, she saw that the name was Graystone Mercantile.

"Your family business?" she asked.

"Indeed. My grandfather became a wealthy man by selling the everyday essentials."

"The Walmart of the last century," she murmured.

"The what?"

"Never mind. Not important." She stepped out of the way of a motorcar that was teetering its way into a side street. A glance downward showed that the asphalt was now rutted dirt. The man behind the wheel of the car said something to the woman beside him and she laughed.

"Can they see us?" Emily whispered to Gabriel, who was now standing beside her.

"Apparently some can and others can't," he replied. "I have spent most of my time avoiding others, trying only to observe."

So, I'd better be careful about stepping out into the road, Emily thought, her heart pounding. She began walking through the market stalls in the center of the Plaza, trying to absorb every detail. Women in stylish dresses strolled past, while men in waistcoats and bowler hats discussed politics—"we're in trouble with that pompous talker, Harding"—and business. Children ran between the stalls, their faces smeared with dirt and joy.

"Gabriel, what should we look for?" she asked, her voice barely audible in the clamor.

"Clues, my dear. Anything that might help us understand the events leading up to my untimely demise," he said, a hint of sadness in his voice.

As they continued through the marketplace, Emily's attention was drawn to a small bakery tucked away in a corner. A sense of familiarity washed over her, reminding her of Sam's little bakery back in her own time.

"Let's go in there," she suggested, pointing to the quaint storefront.

"Very well," Gabriel agreed, his curiosity piqued.

Inside, the aroma of cinnamon and sugar enveloped them. Shelves lined with fresh loaves of bread and pastries greeted them, and behind the counter stood a middle-aged woman with kind eyes and flour-dusted hands.

"Hello," the woman said, a warm smile on her face, obviously able to see them. "What can I get for you today?"

"Uh, hello," Emily stammered, startled by the interaction. "I would like a cinnamon roll, please."

"Of course, dear," the woman replied, eyeing Emily's unusual attire as she handed her the pastry wrapped in waxed paper.

I guess they don't see women in jeans in this day and age. I should find something less obvious to wear.

"Thank you," Emily said, her fingers tingling as they brushed against the woman's hand.

She handed her a quarter, which the woman examined a bit closely, and declined the coins the lady offered as change.

"Keep an eye out," Gabriel whispered in her ear as they

exited the bakery. "You never know what secrets might be hiding in plain sight."

Emily tore off a piece of the cinnamon roll and popped it into her mouth, the sweetness transporting her back to her own time for a brief moment. She glanced around the market, feeling the vibrant life of history everywhere, as if her grandfather's research books had come alive right in front of her.

"Gabriel," she confided, swallowing another bite of her treat, "I can't help but feel like there's something big we're meant to find here, something that will change everything."

His eyes scanned the crowd. "I hope so. Maintain diligence." He took her elbow and guided her down the sidewalk.

They'd barely reached the entrance to the La Fonda when the doors flew open and two men stomped out. They wore dark suits, shirts with high collars and gold cufflinks, and string ties. Their dark hair was recently barbered and both wore neatly trimmed goatees. Emily could tell the fabrics were expensive and they carried themselves with an aura of wealth.

"Maldonados," Gabriel muttered under his breath. His hand went to the holster on his hip.

"Are they—"

The taller of the men noticed them and stopped in his tracks. "Graystone." His eyes shifted to Emily, appraising her from head to toe, his gaze turning to ice.

Gabriel stepped away from Emily, prepared to confront the men.

The second man nudged his brother. "There's nothing to say, Antonio. Let's go."

Emily edged along the front of the hotel, not turning

her back on any of them. Was this the moment of some previous confrontation?

But the others turned abruptly, walking away as if they owned the street. For all she knew, maybe they did. She grabbed Gabriel's arm and tugged him along behind her as she raced into the hotel and through the lobby. Heads turned but she ignored them all.

Somewhere beyond the kitchen was a root cellar and therein would be another tunnel entrance. She could only hope and pray that this one would take her back through the time portal and into her own life.

Chapter 16

Emily was panting when she emerged into the library and shoved the bookcase back in place. Somewhere along the way, as she dashed through the tunnels, Gabriel had vanished, leaving her alone and scared. All she could do was keep running. She looked around, relieved to see her grandfather's books and papers exactly as she'd left them. She was back in her own time.

Bright sunlight streamed through the windows, highlighting the dust motes she'd just disturbed. What on earth? Had she been gone all night?

As for the tunnel and the portal to the past, other than knowing the Maldonados were very much present in Taos in the 1920s, and that there was some underlying tension between them and Gabriel, she had no answers to the mystery. Frustration gripped her.

She took a deep breath and decided she needed coffee. Now. She got out her small French press. She'd no sooner filled the kettle with water and turned it on than she heard a noise. Peering out the front windows, she spotted Kelly's car in the small parking area. Emily yanked the front door open and dragged her friend inside.

"Em, what's up? You look like you've seen a gho— No. I've seen you after you've seen a ghost, and this is worse."

Emily managed a chuckle. "I guess so. Can you stay for a cup of coffee or tea? The water's on."

"Sure. Ana's spending the day with a friend." Kelly trailed her into the back room and the small cart where Emily kept her little beverage bar. "Okay, tell me."

"Gabriel was here and we went down into the tunnels. Kel, it's a time portal. We were back in the 1920s. It felt like I was gone an hour or so, but at least eight hours went by."

"Holy sh—! No way!"

"Way. I need you to believe me on this."

"Oh, I do. I can see it on your face that this is not made up." Kelly accepted a mug and the two of them walked back to the library table where Emily had dropped her backpack.

She reached into it and pulled out the map of the tunnels. She spread it out and showed her friend where the library connected to it, where she believed they had come out near the mercantile store, and where they'd dashed through the hotel to go back below ground.

Kelly traced her fingers along the worn map between them, her green eyes narrowing as she considered the network of tunnels that snaked beneath Taos.

"Mom always said there was more to this town than meets the eye," Kelly mused. "Do you think the tunnels could be related to the Graystone murder?"

Emily bit her lip, her blue eyes clouded with uncertainty. "I'm not sure. But we do know that Gabriel Graystone is familiar with them, right? So it seems likely that they're connected somehow. I suppose this underground network could be a way that the killer managed to sneak up on him that night."

"Should we ask Mom for help?" Kelly asked. "She might have some insights, and maybe the carved box could help us figure this out."

Emily tucked a strand of hair behind her ear. "I think that's a good idea. I trust her judgment." She set down her empty mug. "Give me twenty minutes to shower and I'll be ready to go."

"Let's meet at the bakery," Kelly suggested, pushing back her chair and standing up.

The two women found Samantha in the bakery kitchen, finishing a batch of cupcakes, which she handed off to Jen to put in the display case. Her short gray hair framed her face as she greeted her daughter and Emily warmly.

"Sam, do you have a few minutes?" Emily asked, glancing around the kitchen, not wanting to say too much.

Sam tilted her head toward the back door and they stepped outside. "Sorry. This time of morning is a little crazy here. The whole crew is busy, but if it's something you want to discuss in private …"

Kelly piped up. "Em had a really strange experience last night. In the tunnels. We're trying to make sense of everything, and we were hoping you might have some ideas."

Sam glanced up and down the empty alley behind her business. "Yeah, definitely, we need to catch up. I've got to show you something I discovered in one of the documents you brought over yesterday. This definitely goes beyond coincidence."

"The bakery isn't the best place," Kelly said.

"Right. Let me get some things and we can meet back at Emily's—if that's okay?"

Emily nodded. "Absolutely. Any time."

"Give me an hour?" Sam suggested.

It didn't take nearly that long for Sam to organize the workload at Sweet's Sweets and get back to Emily's place. Em ushered everyone into her warm and cozy kitchen where she had fresh coffee brewed, and they settled at the table. Emily recounted the tale of her trip into the tunnels and the unnerving encounter with the Maldonado brothers.

"Interesting," Sam said after taking it all in. "I had my own little meeting with some modern-day Maldonados yesterday afternoon." She brought out a list she'd made of the names she discovered on the backs of the old family photos. "I didn't get a chance to snap pictures of those old photos, and it didn't seem right to ask to borrow them, considering I'd just met the people."

Emily wondered what was the significance.

Sam pulled a piece of paper from her bag. "I found this name in one of the old records—Iris Maxwell. *And* ... hers was one of the names I found among the Maldonado family photos. When I saw that, I went home and did a little research. Iris Maxwell is still alive."

"What? She has to be a hundred," Emily said.

"One hundred twenty," Sam informed them. "She's on the official record as the oldest living person in New Mexico."

"No kidding! Is she ... I mean, at that age ... Is she

coherent enough to talk to us?"

"I have no idea about that," Sam said, "but she still lives here in Taos, in the same home she's had for decades."

"Should we pay her a visit?" Kelly asked, exchanging a glance with Emily.

"Maybe," Sam replied cautiously. "But I should warn you that she might not be too forthcoming with information about the Graystones. I've heard some rumors around town that she's a bit … eccentric."

"Um, what do you mean?"

"She has the reputation of being a *bruja*," Sam said.

Emily raised an eyebrow. "A witch?"

"You mean, like whatshername …"

"Bertha Martinez, the woman who bequeathed me the wooden box," Sam finished.

Emily knew her expression conveyed her complete puzzlement, and Sam filled her in on the whole story of how, in a supposedly abandoned house, she'd encountered a dying woman who seemed to know she was coming along and wanted her to take possession of this artifact.

"People said Bertha was a *bruja*, too. I never got the chance to speak to her about the box. She died right after that. So, what I know about how to use the box has come about by experimenting. Kind of the ultimate in on-the-job-training, I guess."

"And Iris Maxwell may have similar powers?" Kelly asked, her eyes going wide.

Sam shrugged. "No way to know."

"Still, it's worth a shot to go visit her," Emily said. "If she knows something about the Graystones that could help us solve this mystery, we have to try."

"All right," Sam said, nodding. "I have her address. Just

remember that we need to be cautious, and don't push her too hard if she seems reluctant to talk."

As they prepared to leave, Emily couldn't help but feel a mix of excitement and trepidation. She hoped they were one step closer to solving the Graystone mystery, but what secrets would they learn?

Only time would tell.

Chapter 17

Emily gripped the steering wheel of her Wrangler tightly as she navigated the twisting, narrow roads that wound up the rocky hillside outside Taos. Kelly was in the passenger seat, her eyes scanning the landscape for any sign of their destination. Samantha sat in the back, holding the carved wooden box on her lap as she peered out the window, observing the iffy roadway. Her hope, in bringing along the artifact, was that it might give some insight as to whether this Iris Maxwell had valid information to share.

"Are you sure this is the right way?" Emily asked, her voice tense as she approached a particularly sharp bend in the road.

"According to the directions we have, it should be just ahead," Kelly replied, keeping her gaze fixed on the arid landscape with sparse piñon, cedar, and chamisa stretching out before them.

As they rounded the bend, a small, isolated house came into view. Its adobe exterior was weather-beaten and worn, suggesting years of exposure to the harsh elements of the New Mexico high desert. The trio exchanged glances, each silently wondering what they would find inside. Sam tucked the wooden box into her backpack purse and zipped it safely inside.

"Here goes nothing," Emily muttered under her breath as she parked the Jeep, unbuckled her seatbelt, and stepped out onto the dusty ground.

The three women approached the house cautiously, the dry wind whipping at their hair and clothes. As they reached the front door, Emily took a deep breath and knocked hesitantly.

"Who's there?" called out a frail, slightly shaky voice from within.

The door creaked open, pulled inward by a young woman wearing bright pink scrubs. "I'm Sophie," she said, "Iris's caregiver."

"Is she up to having visitors for a few minutes?" Sam asked.

Sophie cocked her head, evidently assessing whether the ladies were selling something or were here socially. "She loves having new faces around."

She stepped aside to reveal an elderly woman with piercing black eyes that seemed to take in everything at once. She stood near a Victorian era couch, and moved gingerly toward them, aided by the use of a cane. Despite her age, there was a sharp edge behind those eyes that reminded the trio why they were here.

"Hello, Miss Maxwell," Samantha greeted warmly,

attempting to ease the tension. "My name is Samantha Sweet, and these are my daughter and her friend, Kelly and Emily. Emily's family founded the Morton Library in town, and we came across your name. We were hoping we could talk to you about the Graystone family."

Iris Maxwell scrutinized them for a moment before nodding. "Come in, then," she said, her voice holding a hint of suspicion. "Sophie will make us some tea."

As they followed Iris into her modest living room, Emily couldn't help but wonder … would this woman be willing to divulge any information about the Graystones? And if she did, how reliable would the information be, or what secrets might they uncover?

"Please, have a seat," Iris said, gesturing to the worn but comfortable-looking sofa. The trio sat down, making small talk about long-time residents of Taos, waiting for Sophie to return with the tea.

"Here we are," Iris announced, when her caregiver returned with a steaming teapot and a tray of mismatched cups. She poured the tea and handed each of them a cup before settling into an armchair across from them.

"Thank you," Emily murmured, taking a cautious sip of the hot liquid. The warmth spread through her body, providing a momentary sense of comfort in the tense atmosphere.

"All right," Iris said, her eyes flicking between the three women. "What is it you want to know about the Graystones?"

"Miss Maxwell," Sam began, her voice gentle yet determined. "We've come across some mysterious events surrounding the Graystone family, particularly Gabriel Graystone, and we were hoping you might be able to shed some light on their history. Gabriel died at a very young age, and some say his spirit is present in town."

Iris hesitated, her hands tightening around her teacup as she stared into its depths. "The Graystones were a complicated family," she said at last, her voice barely above a whisper.

For several minutes she sat there, not expanding on that statement.

"Please, Iris," Kelly implored, leaning forward earnestly. "Anything you can share could help us. We want to find out who killed Gabriel and why the family suddenly left town."

As Emily watched the exchange, she couldn't help but feel a growing sense of unease. Why was Iris so reluctant to speak of them? Maybe Kelly had said too much?

"All right," Iris sighed, her black eyes flicking from one woman to another. "The Graystones were a prominent family in Taos since Anglos settled in the area. They always seemed to have a hand in everything, from land deals to politics. But they also had their enemies—the Maldonados, for instance. The two families feuded for decades."

That answered the question about whether Gabriel's rejection of Clara had caused the feud. It didn't.

"Feuded over what?" Emily asked, her curiosity piqued.

"Land ownership, mostly," Iris explained. "But there were other issues as well. Rumors of dark magic being used by the Graystones to achieve their goals."

Emily blinked in surprise; her mind immediately drawn to the ghostly figure of Gabriel Graystone. He had said 'trust the magic.' Could it be true that the Graystones possessed otherworldly powers? She shook her head. Gabriel may be appearing to her as a ghost, but that didn't necessarily mean magic was involved. If he had such powers, wouldn't he have solved his own murder?

Sam raised an eyebrow. "Are you certain?"

"Nothing is ever certain with the Graystones," Iris replied cryptically. "But there have been too many strange occurrences for them to be mere coincidences."

"Like the tunnels under the Plaza," Kelly murmured, a thoughtful look in her eyes.

"Exactly," Iris agreed, nodding slowly. "The Graystones were always secretive about those tunnels. Some say they used them for rituals and ceremonies, others believe they led to hidden chambers where the family stored their wealth."

Emily's mind wandered for a moment. Was this how Gabriel had known that the tunnels could transport a person through time? And his mysterious ways, how he would smile and give enigmatic answers. It was clear that there was far more to the story than she had initially realized.

"Is there anything else you can share about the Graystones, Iris?" Sam asked, her gaze focused on the elderly woman. "Anything that might help us understand their connection to the Maldonados?"

"Hm … maybe." Iris hesitated, her hands trembling ever so slightly as she took a sip of tea. "But I'm not sure how much of it is true or just town gossip."

"Please tell us whatever you know," Kelly urged. "We're trying to uncover the truth behind a murder and bring justice to those responsible."

Iris let out a dry chuckle. "Those responsible? You assume they still live."

Sam tilted her head in acknowledgement. "We realize that. But we would like to know more."

Iris seemed to weigh her options for a moment before nodding slowly. "Very well," she sighed, setting her teacup down with a clatter. "The feud between the Graystones and the Maldonados didn't start with Gabriel's murder. It goes back much further than that."

"Do you know what started it?" Sam asked.

Iris shifted in her chair, her eyes avoiding theirs.

"Please? Anything you can tell us would be helpful," Emily said.

The old woman rubbed her gnarled hands together, taking her time. Was she hiding something? Or was her memory failing her due to her age? Whatever the reason, it was clear that they'd need to tread carefully if they were to get the truth out of her.

"All right. Long ago, in the late 1880s, the Graystones and Maldonados had a bitter dispute over land ownership," Iris continued, her voice wavering slightly. "It was common knowledge in town. My parents spoke of it when I was a child. Both families claimed rights to a valuable piece of land near the outskirts of town. It was rumored that an old mine on the property still held large deposits of gold. The men in both families made threats against each other. The land office was faced with making a decision between two seemingly valid deeds. The matter was about to go to court when the situation escalated."

"Over what?" Sam asked.

"A tragic event occurred—the death of a young Maldonado girl."

"Wait, what happened to her?" Emily asked, her curiosity piqued.

"Nobody knows for certain," Iris admitted, her black eyes clouding with sadness. "Some say the Graystones were responsible, while others believe it was merely an accident. Regardless, the incident only served to deepen the hatred between the families."

"Could this land dispute have anything to do with the tunnels?" Sam inquired, her eyes narrowing as she considered the possibility.

"Perhaps," Iris mused, her brow furrowed in thought. "It began before my time, but I heard that the tunnels were built around the same time that the feud started."

"What else can you tell us about the death of the young girl?" Kelly asked, sensing that they might be onto something important.

"Unfortunately, not much more," Iris sighed, her shoulders slumping with weariness. "The details have been lost to time, and both families have done their best to bury the truth. All I know for certain is that the feud between the Graystones and Maldonados shaped the history of Taos in permanent ways."

As Iris's words hung heavy in the air, Emily realized that the complication of land rights and the possibility of gold on the property would have tangled the web of anger and deceit that existed between the two families.

"You're telling us that the Graystones and Maldonados were enemies," Emily mused, "so why would the families want to see a marriage between Gabriel and Clara Maldonado if the parents hated each other?"

Iris shook her head, her wrinkled face turned hard, her mouth set in a firm line. Sophie, who had been hovering at the edge of the room, stepped closer and placed a hand on the old woman's shoulder.

Emily shook her head in disbelief, her blonde hair swaying slightly with the movement. "I can't believe I never knew about any of this land feud," she murmured. "My family has lived here for generations. I'll have to dig further into the records my grandfather saved."

"Sometimes," Iris said, her black eyes locked onto Emily's, "the darkest secrets are hidden right beneath our feet."

Chapter 18

Ashiver ran down Emily's spine at Iris's words. She felt as if the old woman knew much more about this hidden world. Her reference to the Graystones' use of dark magic, the death of a child, the unlikely engagement between Gabriel and Clara.

"Wait," Kelly interjected, her green eyes narrowing in thought. "If the tunnels were connected to the land dispute … could there still be something important hidden in one of them?"

"Perhaps," Iris mused, pausing to sip her tea. "There are whispers that the Graystones hid their most valuable possessions in a secret underground chamber."

"An underground chamber? In the tunnels?" Sam echoed, her eyes widening with fascination.

Iris shrugged her thin shoulders. "No one knows."

Emily's mind raced as she processed this new piece of information. A hidden chamber filled with the Graystones' wealth could hold the key to the motive for Gabriel's death and his connection to the Maldonado brothers.

"Thank you, Iris," Emily said, her voice filled with gratitude. "You've given us a lot to think about."

"Think nothing of it, dear," Iris replied, an enigmatic smile tugging at the corners of her lips. "Just promise me that you'll be careful. The past has a way of haunting us all, and I fear that digging too deep into the Graystone family's secrets may unleash something none of you are prepared to face."

Sam reassured her as they stood up to leave. But inwardly, she hoped Iris's warning was nothing more than the mistrust of an old woman. As the trio made their way back to the Jeep, the sun was sinking low behind the extinct volcanos in the west.

"Well!" Emily breathed, her eyes wide with excitement. "That was enlightening. I actually never thought we'd learn so much about the Graystone family today."

"Neither did I," Sam agreed. "But now that we have this new information, I wonder if there's any way we could find that underground chamber."

"Did you get the impression that this chamber is somewhere within the tunnel system, or was it connected with the Graystone residence?" Emily asked.

"Maybe we should take a look at the town planning office and see if we can get building plans for Graystone Manor," Kelly suggested. "It would be amazing to see if a hidden room is shown on them."

"We'll be too late to do it today," Sam said with a glance at the time. "They'll be closing up about now. But I can stop in there tomorrow at some point."

"Good idea," Emily replied, buckling her seatbelt as she started the engine. "I'd be surprised if the tunnels were that extensive. The old Graystone mansion is more than a mile from the plaza. The tunnels I saw there only seem to connect the shops. I'd say we need to find a way to verify if there's a hidden room at the mansion."

She turned the Jeep around and headed down the mountainside, into the twilight, eager to get back to the library and see what more she could learn about the Graystone family's interesting, perhaps dark, past.

"Right," Kelly said, her jaw set. "The answers we're looking for could be hidden somewhere inside the mansion. We can't afford to waste any time."

"Okay, let's talk strategy," Sam suggested. "A 'chamber' suggests a fairly large room. From what you've said about the tunnels, it seems they are mostly narrow corridors. We need to study the tunnel maps further, to figure out where this chamber might have been, keeping in mind it's likely been sealed off or hidden by now."

"Maybe we should look for any signs of paranormal activity around the area—in the tunnels or the manor house," Emily proposed, remembering Samantha's mystical abilities. "*If* the Graystones were using magic like Iris said, there could be some residual energy that might give us a clue."

"Good idea," Sam agreed, her eyes narrowing in thought. "I think we need to use the wooden boxes to gather our own energy before we tackle this. Speaking of which … I had this with me," she said, holding up the box she had stashed in her bag, "and I didn't get any vibes like that at Iris's house."

"What do you think that means?" Kelly asked. "Maybe she's just too old, has lost her *bruja* mojo, or whatever you'd call it."

"Could be that. Could be the rumors about Iris Maxwell being a witch were only that—rumors."

"And what about her statements about the Graystones using magic?" Kelly seemed skeptical. "That could be completely bogus, too."

They all stared ahead out the windshield for a minute or two, thinking.

"So, what next?" Emily asked, not wanting to speculate about those other sorts of elements at this point.

Sam spoke up. "I'll get over to County Records and see what plans and plot maps I can get for Graystone Manor. Emily, you have the map of the tunnels and you can also show us where they go. Kel, bring the book of runes with you. We never know what that will tell us, but it's been immensely helpful in the past."

"Sounds like a plan," Kelly chimed in, her voice filled with enthusiasm. "I can't wait to head out."

"Let's not get ahead of ourselves," Sam warned gently, though she couldn't hide her own sense of anticipation. "I have a feeling we still have a long way to go before we can solve this case. We'll tackle it first thing in the morning. It'll give us time to prepare and make sure we're ready for whatever we find down there."

Chapter 19

Beau was on the back deck when Sam arrived home, and he waved at her through the French doors, pointing at the grill. Apparently, steak was on the menu tonight. She smiled at his thoughtfulness, dropped her pack on the end of the sofa, and walked out to join him.

"Just getting this fired up," he said, giving her a kiss. "I wasn't sure how long to set the microwave timer for baked potatoes."

"It doesn't take long. I'll do that when I go back in." She breathed in the crisp evening air, clearing her mind, noting the tinge of woodsmoke. In another month, many of the homes out here in the country would be relying on their woodstoves for heat. "How about a salad with this?"

"I'm a little ahead of you on that," he said. "It's made and chilling in the fridge."

"Did I ever tell you, you're the best?"

"You might have mentioned it once or twice." This time the kiss wasn't merely a peck on the cheek.

They walked back into the kitchen together, where she started the potatoes and he seasoned the steaks. She filled him in on her day—Emily's tale about going into the tunnels below the Plaza and their subsequent visit to Iris Maxwell. When the steaks were medium rare, they carried their plates to the dining table and settled in.

"I've been hearing more and more about this Graystone Manor," Sam said. "Do you know anything about it?"

He finished chewing a bite. "Only what I've heard. Never been out there."

"It was built by the Graystone family, sometime in the late 1800s, early 1900s, I think?"

"Yeah. Land developer … or some kind of mining interests, was what I recall. It was owned by a rich family, but whether those were Graystones or someone else, I don't remember. The place was abandoned for some years around the time of the Great Depression and second World War. Maybe longer than that."

Which fit with what they'd heard about the Graystones leaving Taos after Gabriel died.

Sam thought maybe she could find out about other owners, another question to be researched at the county records. "Don't I recall it being open as a business at some point?"

"Um, yeah." He stabbed a cherry tomato out of his salad. "A bed and breakfast. That was about the time I came to town. I don't remember exactly when it quit being that. It probably sat empty for some more years. Gosh, there were big gaps of time between owners. The main one

I remember was maybe fifteen, twenty years ago. Height of the tech boom and there were all these sudden millionaires, and one of them bought the mansion. Spent an absolute fortune refurbishing it top to bottom."

"I kind of remember that too. Not that the guy and his wife ever really assimilated into Taos's social life. Darryl commented that he'd kind of ticked off the local contractors and building suppliers by bringing everything in from California, not using local workers. I wonder whatever happened to them, cause I don't think anyone's living there now."

"Yeah, you're right about that. Either the dotcom bust or the crypto debacles or something like that got him. Scuttlebutt around the department was that he lost everything and left town in the night. One of those." He finished the last bit of his potato. "Why do you ask?"

"It may be the stuff of legends, but we heard that the Graystone family had a huge underground chamber either somewhere in the tunnels or beneath the house and they'd stashed their wealth there."

Beau chuckled as he stood to clear the plates. "Yeah, I'd say that definitely sounds like a legend. Besides, after that many different owners and renovations, what are the odds of finding anything connected to the Graystones out there?"

"I'm sure you're right. It would be crazy to think so." Sam carried the salad bowl and they walked into the kitchen.

"But you're still trying to figure out what's behind the murder of this son …"

"Gabriel. Yes, we're hoping to get some answers." She didn't mention Emily's insistence that she'd met the ghost and conversed with him on several occasions.

Beau stacked the plates in the sink and turned to the freezer. "Ice cream? It's chocolate chip cookie dough."

"Absolutely." She quickly loaded the dishwasher while he scooped the dessert into bowls. All the while, her thoughts were running over the conversation this afternoon with Iris Maxwell. Was it somehow possible that the tunnels and the Graystone mansion were connected, and how would she find out? Her mind turned to the carved wooden box and book of runes. Maybe therein would lie some answers.

Chapter 20

Emily rolled over in bed for the tenth time. Her mattress felt like rock, and the covers tangled around her legs. The old woman's words kept echoing through her head. She finally gave up on sleep and slipped out from under the covers, shivering as her toes touched the cold wooden floor. Wrapping herself in a light kimono, she decided to explore some more in the library to clear her head.

"Gabriel?" Emily called softly, as she switched on the light. Her eyes scanned the room, finally finding him standing by the tall bookshelves that lined the west walls.

"Ah, Emily," he said, his voice gentle as if sensing her apprehension. "Can't sleep? I'm not surprised after everything that's happened."

"Neither am I." She hesitated, biting her lip, before continuing. "I wanted to ask you something. I heard that your family once practiced some kind of dark magic. Is that true?"

His expression remained bland. "Remember that I was not much more than a lad, Emily. I do not know everything my parents did to accumulate their wealth."

That didn't exactly answer her question, but she at least got the feeling his answer was truthful, as far as it went. "One more thing. Would you ... could we go back down to the tunnels?"

Gabriel raised an eyebrow, although he didn't seem very surprised by her request. "You want to go down there now? It's late. What's driving you to do this?"

Emily sighed, bracing herself for his reaction. "Our last trip through the tunnels gave me a feel for the layout, but only of a few places. And we didn't find the answer to our main question. I still need to know what happened to you, Gabriel. You asked for my help and we need to uncover the truth about your death. I've been thinking about it all night, and I feel sure there's something we've missed."

Gabriel was silent for a moment, seemingly weighing the risks against his own desire for answers. Finally, he spoke. "All right, Emily. I shall accompany you. But we must be careful."

"Thank you," she breathed, relief washing over her. Together, they descended the worn stone steps behind the bookcase and the underground path that led them into the hidden tunnels, her flashlight beam cutting through the darkness.

As they ventured farther, Emily felt again the strange connection to the past, and she could almost hear the whispers of long-forgotten secrets echoing through the narrow passageways.

"Gabriel," Emily said, her voice barely audible. "When we find out who's responsible for your death, what will you do?"

Gabriel paused, his face somber in the dim light. "I don't know, Emily. I suppose it depends on how much I learn, and whether or not I can make peace with it."

Emily understood his need for closure. She just hoped they would find the answers and that those answers wouldn't bring more pain than he could bear.

"Let's keep moving," Gabriel urged.

The dusty air clung to Emily's skin as she and Gabriel came to a bend in the tunnel, the flashlight casting eerie shadows on the walls. She had the feeling that they were being watched, as if the past itself had eyes.

"Look at this," Gabriel said suddenly, pointing to an inscription carved into the tunnel wall. As Emily leaned closer to examine it, she felt a surge of energy course through her body, and the world around her seemed to shift.

"Gabriel, what's happening?" she gasped, gripping his arm. The flashlight flickered; a strong gust of wind ruffled their hair.

"We've traveled back in time again," Gabriel whispered, "That inscription on the wall, the carving I touched, must be one of the magical artifacts my grandmother spoke of."

So there was magic, of some kind, in the Graystone family.

When the light returned, she heard music. Lively jazz seemed to be coming from the small branch of the tunnel to their right. A set of steps with a wooden door at the top indicated the entrance to one of the Plaza shops. But when they climbed and opened the door, they found themselves in a bustling speakeasy. Women in fringed flapper dresses—with feathered headbands, long strands of pearls, and cigarette holders—stood at a bar, flirting openly with men in striped suits and spats.

"Are you kidding me?" Emily muttered, taking in the scene around her. "I don't recognize this place." Privately, she wondered if they would figure out a way back in time as easily as on their previous trip down.

"Let's look for clues first," Gabriel suggested, his curiosity piqued. "We might find something here that could help us find my killer."

"Okay." He was right. They'd come down into the tunnel for this purpose, and this might be their best chance ever. They cautiously moved into the crowded speakeasy, trying not to draw attention to themselves.

"Hey, isn't that Augustine Maldonado?" Emily whispered, spotting a man with slicked-back dark hair and sharp features sitting at the far end of the bar. She recalled seeing his face in one of her grandfather's old photo albums, and the man fit the description Sam had given.

"Yes," Gabriel confirmed, his gaze following Emily's. "He seems to be arguing with the man next to him, the one with his back to us. Can you get closer and listen? I can't risk him seeing me."

He edged into a dark corner of the room and sat at a tiny table, pulling his hat low over his forehead.

Emily studied the crowd, keeping her eyes on Augustine Maldonado while trying to turn her back well enough that he wouldn't notice her, and painfully aware that she'd come down here wearing her night clothes. She slipped her kimono off and used the belt to tie low around the waist of her cotton nightgown. It wasn't any glamorous flapper dress, but it more closely resembled the dropped-waist style of the day. She fluffed her hair and slung the robe over her arm, casually snagging a glass from the bar when no one was looking. Now the trick was to avoid eye contact with anyone.

"Stay alert, Emily," Gabriel whispered to her. "We can't stay here too long. Someone might recognize me, and I have no idea what would happen."

"Promise me we'll leave as soon as we find what we're looking for," Emily said, her eyes meeting his. He nodded solemnly, acknowledging the danger they faced in this unknown world.

"Deal," he agreed quietly.

She edged toward Maldonado and tuned her ear toward the conversation, which was growing louder by the minute.

"… owe me five thousand dollars," the other man was saying. "And I'm not leaving until I get it."

Maldonado's response was to laugh. "It won't happen, my man. This was Antonio's deal, and I'm sorry but you made a bad choice. The deal flopped, years ago. There's nothing for the investors, including myself and my family."

Emily sneaked a closer look at the man who was making the assertion. He bore a certain resemblance to Gabriel. His brother?

He looked up just then and she spun on her heel to keep him from noticing her. A hand slammed down on the bar and a stool screeched across the wooden floor.

"This is not the last of the matter!" the man shouted. He rushed past her, bumping her shoulder with a force that felt very real.

From the corner of her eye, she could see that Maldonado was watching as the other man stomped away from the bar and left the room. She edged her way back to

Gabriel's corner.

"Did you see that man, the one arguing with Maldonado?"

"Barely. It's clear across the room and it's very smoky in here." That much was true.

"Did you recognize him?"

He shook his head.

"Let's see if we can follow. I want you to identify him, if you can," she said, pulling at his coat.

But by the time they crossed the crowded speakeasy and made their way to the door where he'd exited, the man was long gone. Emily debated about asking Gabriel if it could have been his brother, but already he'd said he was too far away to recognize the man. She briefly told him that the argument seemed to be about an outstanding debt, perhaps to someone who had invested in a Maldonado business.

"Does that ring a bell, um, sound familiar to you?" she asked.

"Perhaps. In my time there were a lot of deals being made, a lot of people wanting to invest and make a killing in mines and many other things."

She sighed. He was right. This was the Roaring Twenties. Before the stock market crash and Great Depression, people had money and many of them were throwing it around pretty wildly. The two men might have been discussing almost any type of business deal that didn't pan out the way one of them wanted.

"Okay, you're right. Let's find our way back to my time."

* * *

The musty air sent an icy chill down Emily's spine, and she slipped her kimono back on, redoing the belt tightly. The light from her flashlight reflected off the damp earthen walls, casting eerie shadows that danced with each step they took, but it was beginning to dim.

She felt an edge of panic that they might be trapped in the dark. She should have brought two flashlights or some extra batteries as backup. She shook the flashlight and it brightened again.

"Let's find an exit," she suggested. "We may not have a lot more light down here."

He led the way down a long stretch where the walls felt close. She imagined the map in her mind and thought they may have traversed beneath the entire length of the Plaza to where the modern-day Bent Street shops were.

"Gabriel," Emily suddenly spoke up, breaking the silence that had settled between them. "Why did you break off your engagement with Clara Maldonado? I mean, if you were in love …"

He sighed, his ghostly breath leaving a faint mist in the air. "As you know, my family and the Maldonados had a bitter feud going back fifty years. I loved Clara but this was a constant source of tension, and I knew that marrying her would only make things worse. My family was opposed to the marriage but the Maldonados were pushing us together. It was all about money for them. For my family, the goal was political power. For me, I wanted to live on the land and do my artwork."

For a moment, Emily considered the weight of such a decision, trying to imagine what it must have been like for Gabriel to be pulled between his family and the woman he loved.

"Clara's brothers, Augustine and Antonio, they never forgave me for the breakup," Gabriel continued. "I suspect they had a hand in my death. Keep an eye on them as we continue our search. They're dangerous men."

"All right," Emily replied. "But I need to know more about what happened on the day you died."

"Very well," Gabriel agreed reluctantly. "That morning, I met with Clara in secret. I wanted to tell her in person that we shouldn't go through with the marriage. She was devastated, of course, but she understood my reasoning."

Emily listened intently, her heart aching for the tragic love story that had been cut short so abruptly.

"Late that evening, I was walking home when it happened," Gabriel continued, his voice laced with pain. "I don't remember my attacker, but I felt a sharp, searing pain in my chest, and then ... nothing."

"I wonder if Clara ever suspected her brothers?" Emily asked, her mind racing as she tried to piece together the information they had collected so far.

"Clara had told me Augustine and Antonio would be furious about the broken engagement," Gabriel replied. "But I don't think she could ever imagine they'd go as far as murder. She loved them too, despite their flaws."

They came to another bend in the tunnel, an intersection where the choice was to turn left or right. Emily cast the dim glow of her flashlight on the walls; eerie shadows leapt at her. She shivered, her breath visible in the chilly air, and gripped Gabriel's hand tightly, as if it would tether her to this world against the pull of the past.

"Listen," Gabriel whispered, holding up a hand and facing the left-hand turn. Emily strained to hear, and at the edge of her perception, she caught the faintest strains of music, laughter, and clinking glasses. It sounded like a party from long ago, almost drowned out by the passage of time itself.

"Is that another speakeasy?" she asked.

Gabriel's gray eyes looked haunted. "Yes, I think so. I also think we're close to where it all happened."

She could swear she saw the edges of a woman's flapper dress disappear around the bend. Facing the other choice, the right-hand turn, she thought she heard the distant rumble of an old car engine.

"Gabriel, these tunnels..." she murmured, her voice tinged with awe. "They really are a window into your world."

He smiled sadly, giving her hand a gentle squeeze. "I never thought I'd see it again. But I'm glad I can share it with you, Emily. Let's go this way. Through the speakeasy there must be a way up to the street and back to your time."

Emily's heart pounded in sync with the muffled beat of jazz music that grew louder as they walked. The scent of cigarette smoke and perfume began to mingle with the dusty air, and she felt a strange sense of longing, wondering about a time she'd never known. They came to a wooden door and Gabriel reached to pull it open.

"Wait," Emily whispered suddenly, stopping in her tracks. She shone her flashlight at the wall, illuminating an old newspaper article that had been pasted there. The headline read: **Maldonado Brothers Arrested in Connection with String of Robberies.**

Chapter 21

Sam rolled over in bed and stared at the red numerals on the clock. Barely after one a.m. This was ridiculous. She had a fairly full day at the bakery tomorrow—later today— not to mention her promise to get together with Kelly and Emily to work some more on Emily's newest mystery. A full night's sleep really was not optional.

She slipped quietly from under the covers, taking care not to wake Beau. She'd set the wooden box on top of her dresser, and now she grabbed it and a robe, and headed down the stairs. Ranger and Nellie raised their heads from their beds near the fireplace, but neither of the dogs felt the need to jump up and check on her. She padded into the kitchen and set the kettle on the burner. Maybe a cup of Sleepy Time tea would do the trick.

Five minutes later, snuggled into her favorite corner

of the sofa, she held the box on her lap and placed both hands on its lumpy surface. The wood began to glow, softly golden, warming her hands. She closed her eyes and sent her attention to the question of the day—what was the answer to Emily's dilemma about Gabriel Graystone?

The box warmed. Even with her eyes closed, Sam sensed a glow in the air. One of the dogs whined, but she kept her eyes shut and focused as an image slowly emerged in the darkness. Music came to her, although she would swear it was entirely in her head. Lively jazz. The image sharpened. A crowded bar, a jazz band in the corner. The people were dressed as in the Roaring Twenties. They were dancing the Charleston. Sam's toe began to tap in time with the sound.

In a flash, the music went out of tune. Emily appeared in the image, looking scared, and a slimy looking man at the bar left his stool to follow her.

Sam's eyes snapped open. *What on earth?*

* * *

Kelly unlocked the door to the attic room that was her *sanctum sanctorum*, or so she joked. She'd made the space her own when they moved into the Victorian home, just as Scott had claimed the turret room as his writing space. It was where Kelly kept the book of runes and the wooden box that was nearly a twin to her mother's. No one was allowed in here without her being present. She couldn't take the chance that Ana would accidentally stumble upon something out of her realm.

It was also the place she came when she couldn't sleep and didn't know why.

Life was fine. Scott was on the road, and they'd talked

every evening so he could tell Ana about his day and kiss her goodnight by video. And her little daughter was safely tucked away in her bed, recovering from having spent last night with a friend where they, no doubt, got very little sleep. So what was with the sleepless night?

Kelly turned on the gas fire in her little cast-iron stove, warming the chilly room, and then retrieved the book of runes from its place in the cabinet. Who was she kidding? She knew exactly why she couldn't sleep. Gabriel Graystone and the investigation he'd begged Emily to conduct, which pulled herself and Sam in as well.

And she didn't mind that, truly. She loved looking into anything mysterious. She loved the fact that she'd been instrumental in helping to solve several mysteries, including one in England where the mysterious book of runes had come into her possession.

Granted, today had been a full day, with the revelations about the Graystone family and most especially the visit to the old woman who gave off mildly creepy vibes. However, what was keeping her awake now was an edgy feeling, down in her gut, that Emily was somehow in danger.

She took a seat on the stool in front of her worktable. Balancing the book on its spine with her hands pressed flat against the covers, she posed her question: *Where is Emily, and is she in danger?*

When she let go of the covers, the book fell open to a random page and Kelly looked down to see what would be revealed. A feather. A bright pink feather that might have fallen off a fancy dress or hat.

"That's *it?*" Kelly stared, trying to make sense of the message.

Chapter 22

Did you know about this?" Emily asked Gabriel, her voice shaking as she pointed to the newspaper headline.

"No," he replied, his eyes scanning the faded print. "But it makes sense. They were always looking for ways to gain power and control… even if it meant breaking the law."

"But robbery? What would they have to gain by robbing local businesses of cash or goods? If these men owned gold mines and were such big real estate wheeler-dealers, why would they bother with this kind of thing?"

"That, my dear, I cannot answer."

"Maybe the items they stole had some kind of hidden meaning. Could they have killed you for the same reason?" Emily wondered aloud, her thoughts racing ahead to the implications of this new discovery.

"Perhaps," Gabriel mused, his expression pained. "We can't be sure yet. But it's another piece of the puzzle, isn't it?"

"It is," she said, folding up the article and tucking it into her bag. "Where are we now?" she asked, pulling out the crude map of the tunnels. "Can you make a guess?"

She spread out the map and handed it to him while she held the light.

"The speakeasy we entered, where Augustine was arguing with someone … I believe that to be the bar in the hotel. It was a very popular spot in my day." He ran a finger along the drawing, following the path they'd taken when they descended into the tunnel again. "Here is the intersection we just passed, where we heard more of the music."

"Right." Emily could envision where, in the present day, a short walking mall of shops existed.

"So, in that case, I believe we might be beneath Bent Street," he said. "I was killed near the large elm tree. Up the street to the west was a small shop, a dealer in household goods and such, where Clara held a job, right before we were to be married."

Emily's eyes grew wide at this news. "We should go there."

"Are you ready for what we might find?" Gabriel asked softly, sensing Emily's apprehension.

"Are you?" she countered.

"More than anything," he replied, his voice tight with emotion.

As they rounded the next bend, they passed through an archway braced with beams and timbers. Beyond the arch lay a large chamber dimly lit by high clerestory windows and moonlight. They paused, staring.

"Let's do this," Emily said, her voice steady now. Together, they stepped into the unknown space, as her flashlight revealed an amazing array. Packing crates, furniture, a treadle sewing machine, coffee grinders, and two Hoosier cabinets were only a few of the items.

By the look of it, this would probably be a storeroom in the basement of a shop in modern times, Emily thought. The air in the chamber felt heavy with history, every nook and cranny filled with items that, in her time, would be antiques. Grandma Valerie would be in heaven here. Emily's heart raced as she tried to keep her thoughts focused on the task at hand, finding clues in Gabriel's time.

"Look here," Gabriel whispered, pointing to a dusty leather-bound journal resting in the drawer of an old wooden desk. As Emily picked it up, dust swirled through the dim light. She sneezed as it tickled her nose.

"Whose journal is this?" Emily asked, opening the book and flicking through the pages.

"Clara's," Gabriel replied, his voice barely audible. "I never thought we'd find it."

"This must be the shop you mentioned, where she used to work. Maybe she hid it here, thinking it wasn't safe to have it at home."

Her fingers traced over the delicate loops and whorls of Clara's handwriting. The pages almost hummed with energy. She could feel the tension in Gabriel as he stood beside her, his spirit still tethered to this world in so many ways.

"Listen to this entry," Emily said, her voice tinged with awe. "'Augustine and Antonio have gone too far. They've hired Tomas Ramos to kill Gabriel. What should I do? Plead with Tomas? I must. I cannot let them get away with this.'"

"Tomas…" Gabriel murmured, his eyes dark. "He was my friend, and yet he was involved in this plot against me?"

Emily ran her finger down the page, scanning entries, then glancing up at Gabriel. His expression remained tortured.

"More questions than answers," he muttered, running a transparent hand through his hair. "We need to find out what happened between Tomas and my killers."

"Clara doesn't say anything more than what I just read. Could there be more journals?" Emily asked, her blue eyes scanning the dimly lit chamber.

"Perhaps," Gabriel replied, his gaze lingering on the shadows just beyond the reach of their flashlight. "We'll have to keep looking."

"Emily," Gabriel said suddenly, halting in his tracks. "Do you feel that?"

She paused, her own breath held in anticipation. "It feels like … a presence."

"Protective," he whispered. "Like something—or someone—is watching over us, more ghosts of the past, stirring."

"Could it be Clara?" Emily suggested, her mind racing with the possibilities.

"Maybe," Gabriel's eyes never left the darkness that surrounded them. "But we can't lose focus. We need to keep searching for proof of who the real killer was because I cannot believe my friend Tomas was the one."

Chapter 23

In the early morning chill, Emily wrapped her handmade shawl more tightly around her shoulders, then pushed open the door at Michael's Kitchen. She felt the warmth of the room envelop her as she scanned the cozy space for Samantha and Kelly. Sugar-dusted *empanadas* and the scent of coffee embraced her in the tiny lobby.

"Over here, Emily!" Kelly called out, waving from a corner booth. Her curly cinnamon hair framed her face, green eyes sparkling with excitement. Samantha sat across from her, sipping on a steaming mug. Between them, Ana sat with her knees tucked under her as she fiddled with the paper sugar packets.

"Hey, you three!" Emily greeted them, sliding into the booth beside Kelly. "I'm so glad you texted with this plan."

"You won't believe the night I had," said Sam and Kelly

at once. They all laughed.

"What do you mean?" Ana asked, her little face bright with curiosity. "You were home in bed, Mommy."

"I was," Kelly told her daughter, "but I had some strange dreams. In one, I was looking in a book—" she made significant eye contact with Sam "—and the page opened to a realistic sketch of a pink feather."

Ana settled back, picking up her mug of hot chocolate with two hands.

Emily stifled a gasp. Glancing at the child among them, she nodded. "My *vision* contained someone wearing pink feathers on a beaded headband."

"Inside an old-fashioned 1920s type of speakeasy?" Sam asked.

Emily's face said it all.

A harried-looking waitress came over just then and took their orders—pancakes for Ana, breakfast burritos for the others.

When she walked away, Emily pulled out the yellowed slip of paper she had discovered at the hidden underground bar. "It's an old newspaper clipping about the Maldonados and a crime spree. We found it—" She pointed downward.

Samantha leaned forward, focusing on the paper. "Wow, fascinating," she murmured, as she read the fragile newsprint. "I wonder if they went to prison for this or if they managed to get off."

"That would be interesting to know," agreed Kelly, taking a sip of her cappuccino. "There must be some reason Augustine and Antonio Maldonado targeted Gabriel specifically. It was their fathers who were feuding. I'm not sure I buy the whole 'family honor' theory. Seriously, this was the 1920s, not the 1720s. Women were beginning to have lives of their own and their own say in their futures."

Emily stared down at the newspaper article, lost in thought. She remembered the rowdy atmosphere of the speakeasy, the haunting sense of history that lingered within its walls, and the argument between Augustine Maldonado and the other man. What other secrets did those old underground spaces hold?

Their food arrived just then, and conversation dropped off as they cut into the steaming burritos filled with eggs, bacon, potatoes, and cheese, smothered in green chile sauce.

"Maybe we should dig deeper into the Maldonado family," Samantha suggested, breaking the silence a few minutes later. "They were local businessmen in the 1920s, so there could be records of them at the courthouse, in the newspaper archives, or online. If we can learn more about their motivations and connections to the Graystones, we might be able to learn more about this old feud and whether it was motive enough for murder."

"Great idea, Mom," Kelly chimed in. She set her fork down and pulled out her phone. "Why didn't I think of this sooner, right?"

She typed the names into a search engine and waited. "Well, disappointment. At least so far, none of these matches seem to be related to Taos or to the right time period."

"That's probably not surprising," Emily said. "New Mexico is *so* filled with history that it would have been impossible for all of it to be saved for posterity—Taos itself was founded in 1615. A lot of the older events, especially in small towns like this, have never been uploaded to any modern websites. It's one of the reasons my family's library is in such demand by researchers. We have materials that don't exist elsewhere."

"What if we split up and see what we can accomplish?" Sam suggested. "The courthouse records of births and deaths could provide some information."

"I'll take that job," Kelly offered, "if you would like to have Ana help you at the bakery this morning?"

Sam took the hint. "Good plan. Becky and I have a fairly big stack of orders to turn out. Ana can help with the items for the sales counter. You like to put icing on the scones, don't you?"

Ana agreed enthusiastically, her mouth full of pancake.

"Okay, so Kelly will go to the courthouse. Emily, maybe the newspaper offices, take a look through their archives? That article you found would be a good starting place."

"Definitely. I'd like to see if the arrest described here resulted in either of the brothers doing any prison time or if they managed to get off scot-free. Based on their reputation and influence in this county, I wouldn't be surprised if they were both running free at the time Gabriel died." Emily felt a surge of determination. "Let's do it." She tucked the newspaper clipping carefully back into her bag. "Maybe the key to solving Gabriel's murder lies with something that was going on in the Maldonado family."

Samantha smiled warmly, her eyes twinkling as she pulled out a credit card and informed the others that breakfast was her treat. "Justice for Gabriel—that's our task."

It was late morning when Emily walked into the offices of the *Taos News*. She explained her mission to the young man behind the reception desk, probably an intern since he looked no more than twenty. "This clipping is dated 1919, so I'd like to look through the old issues from that year and the following. I assume everything is on microfiche now?"

"Yes, ma'am," he said, standing.

Cute. Ma'am. Did she really look that much older? Twenty-eight was hardly a matronly age … was it?

But she was here on a mission, not to quibble semantics with a guy barely out of his teens. Emily followed him to a tiny square room.

"These are the filmstrips," he said, pointing to a shelf laden with boxes. "And the machine is just there. And in the next room are bound copies of old papers that go way back. You'd need to ask for the key. The boss is kind of picky about handling those, since they're pretty fragile."

"Thanks." She didn't bother to tell him she was well aware of how to handle old documents. She glanced at the dates on the microfilm boxes. "I'll probably be able to find what I need here."

Emily settled into a chair near one of the microfilm machines, carefully threading the reel with expert hands. As the machine hummed to life, she leaned forward, gazing intently at the screen before her. The past stretched out before her, an endless story, each image providing another clue.

"Hmm, interesting," she muttered when she found a later article naming the Maldonado brothers' children. She quickly scanned the piece, in which they maintained their fathers' innocence in Gabriel Graystone's murder. When questioned about their obvious hatred for the Graystones, Antonio's son said there was more to this story than met the eye.

The reporter persisted, Emily learned, scanning the

page as she continued to read. According to the family, there were several instances of the Maldonado children being harassed by the Graystones, but they never retaliated or sought revenge. They just wanted to be left alone.

"That doesn't sound like the Maldonado I overheard in the bar last night," she murmured. "Not like the behavior of a family that's out for blood."

Did the Maldonados have some kind of pull at the newspaper?

Chapter 24

Ana held up a cupcake for Sam's inspection. Although she tried hard, a five-year-old's version of decorative icing didn't quite reach the mark for what they could sell in the shop.

"I'm thinking that one should be your afternoon snack," Sam said. "Ask Jen to make you a hot chocolate to go with it. Mommy should be back in a little while."

How long could a person spend in the vital records department anyway? Sam wondered.

As if in answer to her question, Kelly came through the back door just then. She grabbed Ana in a hug. "Hey, how's it going? Can I have half of that cupcake?"

"Sure, Mommy. Auntie Jen is supposed to make me some hot chocolate to go with it!"

"Maybe we settle for a glass of milk instead of more

sugar?" Kelly moved to the fridge and found the milk carton.

"Sorry, don't know what I was thinking," Sam admitted.

"You forget, I don't have Scott at home to help turn off her energy-button before bedtime," Kelly said with a grin.

"How's the book tour going anyway?"

"Going well, he says. Lots of middle-schoolers who are hooked on his mystery series, and their parents are coming along with money in hand."

"That sounds like a *big* success." Sam wiped down her end of the crowded worktable.

"I just got a text from Emily, asking if we wanted to meet up this afternoon and go over our findings. I'm thinking yes."

"Sure. Here or at the library?"

"Whichever. How busy are you right now?"

Sam looked at the stack of order sheets, which had dwindled during the day. "Becky, what do you think? Can you manage the rest of these if I leave for a while?"

"Absolutely, not a problem. Go." She may have meant 'get Ana away from the sugar' but Sam wasn't sure. Becky was always great with kids around.

"I'll tell Emily we'll meet at her place," Kelly said, pulling her phone from her pocket.

Fifteen minutes later, they'd settled Ana in front of the TV in Emily's home, a favorite video entertaining her, and the three women were in the kitchen with mugs of tea and a few of Sam's special Mexican wedding cookies.

"You go first," Emily told Kelly.

"Well, the main thing I can tell you is that the county isn't nearly as updated as the newspaper. Microfilm? Not hardly. There are rooms full of dusty old books, these huge binders with handwritten records."

"Ugh, not fun."

"Yeah, well, I did find a clerk who was helpful enough to pull the ones from the years we thought were pertinent. She left me alone at a table to page through them. I have to say, a person can get lost in just reading names. I found my mind wandering along the lines of 'I wonder if this person was related to that kid I knew in school' sort of thing. It takes some discipline to stay on track."

"And now you know what I face every single day," Emily said with a laugh, helping herself to another cookie from the box. "It's so hard not to go down the rabbit hole of every single story I come across out in Grandpa's library."

"Anyway, long story short, I did come up with dates of birth and death for each of the Graystones and the Maldonados we know about. I made notes. Tomorrow, I think I may go back and see if the property records indicate who owned what in the way of real estate. We heard that one of the fights between them had to do with a gold claim. And there was the death of the young Maldonado girl. With her birth and death dates, maybe I can find something more in the news." She handed a sheet of paper to each of them, photocopies she'd made of her notes. "For what it's worth."

"This was a lot of work. Thanks, Kel," Sam said, reading through the information. "Em, you got the cushy job of going through microfiche records …"

"Ha-ha. Cushy and eye straining. But yes, I did." She laid a few sheets of copied pages on the table. "The newspaper covered the whole story of Gabriel's death, with the law enforcement reports as the basis, of course. His body was found in the early morning hours on Bent Street, with knife wounds. They didn't have the technology they use today, of course, but with witness accounts from someone who had passed that way around ten p.m. and swore there was not a body on the street at that time, up to the person who reported it to the sheriff around five o'clock the next morning, they got a fairly accurate window of time for the murder to have happened."

Her eyes were damp, and Kelly placed a hand on her arm.

Taking a deep breath, Emily continued. "Gabriel told me he was walking along Bent Street about eleven that night and that's when it happened." Her voice broke a little. She swallowed hard. "Anyway, the news seems to have it fairly accurate. Of course, the first thing law enforcement did was to check out suspects, and the Maldonado name came up right away because the feud was well known. And witnesses had overheard Augustine Maldonado arguing with Gabriel in a bar earlier in the evening."

She looked up. "I witnessed that argument, down in the tunnels last night. It wasn't Gabriel, but someone who looked a lot like him. I think it could have been his brother Nathaniel. I didn't get a close look, but I do know it wasn't Gabriel's voice." She took a sip of her tea and turned back to the printed pages.

"Anyway, back to the news accounts. Both of the Maldonado brothers had alibis that were verified. Someone suggested a hired hit, and they questioned Tomas Ramos for that. Ramos acknowledged he'd been approached by the Maldonados, but he swears he didn't do it. Gabriel told me Tomas was his friend, and although he didn't see his attacker, he didn't believe Tomas would be capable of killing him. The sheriff evidently held Tomas for a while, but we don't know how it turned out. If they'd arrested and tried him, it would have generated a bigger news story than this."

Sam picked up the printed sheets on the table. "You're right. This doesn't seem like a lot of news coverage for what had to be a fairly high-profile murder."

"I know," Emily said, "and I looked through the archives for several weeks after. Even though this was a prominent family, the whole thing just fizzled after they cleared those three main suspects."

"I wonder why," Kelly pondered.

Emily nibbled at her lower lip for a moment. "One factor was probably that a bigger story came along. Same as today. A major story fills our lives for several days, maybe a week or more, then the next big thing comes along and pulls our attention in that direction. In this case, the week after the questioning of Tomas Ramos, the governor visited Taos, and the day after that there was a scandal in the Santa Fe legislature. Pretty soon there was no more mention of Gabriel's case."

"That's just not right," Kelly said.

"I know. And it doesn't mean the sheriff and his men weren't still working the case. But we don't know for sure. Maybe they were innocent after all and we've been on the wrong trail," Emily speculated, her mind racing with possibilities. "But then who killed Gabriel?"

"Perhaps it was someone else entirely, someone we haven't considered yet," Samantha suggested thoughtfully. "A mugging on the street? Surely those things happened back then, too."

"Or maybe we're missing a crucial piece of the puzzle," Kelly added. "The killer could have been someone else hired by the Maldonados."

"Either way, we need to keep digging," Emily said resolutely. "I know there are documents among my great-grandfather's things that I haven't seen yet."

"If I can find someplace for Ana to be for a while tomorrow, I'll go back to the county," Kelly offered. "I'm thinking the property records, tax records, or mineral rights claims … I can't help but think that the battle over the mining claim could be crucial to this."

Sam reminded them, "Beau always says, follow the money."

"Did somebody say my name?" Ana bounded into the kitchen, her movie clearly finished. "Want my help with something?"

Sam grabbed the little girl and pulled her onto her lap. "We might. But for right now, we need to give Emily some time to herself and we'll all go home for dinner."

Chapter 25

Emily stretched lazily in bed, enjoying the tingle to her limbs, the warmth of the duvet, and the chill in the early morning air. It was the first night she'd slept through without a single interruption. No visits from ghosts, no trips down into musty tunnels, and it felt good.

She rolled over and got out of bed, thinking of her options for breakfast as she completed her shower and brushed out her shoulder length hair. A bowl of yogurt and berries, she decided, then she'd better get over to the library. One patron had called, saying he would return some books today, and another wanted a ten a.m. appointment to research Taos Pueblo bread baking techniques. She didn't remind the woman that she could easily drive out to the pueblo and learn all about bread, firsthand. Patrons like these were what kept the private library funded, and she loved them.

And then … once she'd taken care of her patrons, she needed to prowl around in the back room and see what other materials she might find pertaining to Gabriel's case. She set the kettle on the stove, thinking of his face. A person can't fall in love with a ghost, she reminded herself in a stern tone. But Gabriel had that winning combination—a man who needed her help, a kind yet vulnerable streak, not to mention his ruggedly handsome face and what she suspected would be a killer body if dressed in a tight t-shirt that showed off his amazing biceps.

"Stop this," she said out loud. "This whole line of thought is going nowhere, and you will quit it this minute."

"Emily, darling," came a familiar woman's voice, "what are you talking about?"

Emily blushed and turned to see the semi-transparent figure of her grandmother standing in the kitchen doorway.

"Nothing. Nothing at all." She poured boiling water over her favorite Assam tea, then reached into the fridge for a yogurt. "I've been mulling over my latest historical research, that's all."

"And this *research* has a gorgeous face and a hunky body." Valerie laughed. She drifted into the room as Emily sat at the table. "Don't look so shocked. I was a teenager in the '60s. We've all been around the block once or twice."

"Okay, yeah. But do *not* tell anyone."

"Your secret is safe with me." Valerie pursed her mouth and picked at an imaginary cuticle. "Of course I do know how to make ghostly noises in the night."

"Oh shut up," Emily said, laughing out loud. "Hey, you don't happen to know *where* Grandpa would have filed documents pertaining to either the Maldonado or

Graystone families, do you? I know. I'm sounding like a broken record."

Valerie shook her head. "Sorry. That whole library—other than the secret entrance—is outside my realm. The men were the historians in this family, and I was happy to keep my distance. Although you know I would do anything for you, sweetie, and I'd lend a hand if I knew where to find—" With that, her ghostly image disappeared.

Emily finished her breakfast quickly and poured more tea into an insulated mug to take with her. Two minutes later, she arrived at work, smiling and grateful she'd given up city life and a twenty-five-minute morning commute for this.

"Okay," she told herself. "Today I tackle some of those boxes I've never had time for. And I will not get sidetracked by false leads. One track!"

And then the doorbell rang, and she spotted the patron who was here to return books. An hour passed as her two visitors took up more time than she'd budgeted, and a few minutes after ten Kelly showed up.

"I arranged a play date for Ana and got an early start at the county building. It's amazing what you can accomplish without the normal family obligations," she told Emily, breezing in and setting a folder on the front desk.

And it's amazing how, even without a husband or child, the morning can still slip away from me.

"So, I haven't read any of this," Kelly told her, "but what I've got here are copies of property records and mining claims in the names of Graystone or Maldonado. I just had the clerk tell me what books to look in and then she was kind enough to run copies of everything for me."

"You can either sit here at the front desk or library

table, or come with me into the storeroom. I'm determined to tackle more of these older records today, and I have no idea how long that will take. Fair warning—dust is everywhere."

"I'll brave the storeroom with you. I took my allergy pill this morning. Chamisa pollen is crazy out at our house this time of year." Kelly followed along as Emily led the way.

She set her folder on the long worktable and Emily grabbed a box from a shelf. One side bore the label 'Estate Sales 1964.' Grandpa David had once told her that both his father and grandfather had frequented estate sales, garage sales, and thrift shops, almost any place in the region that might prove to be a great source for old documents. Clearly, no one in three generations had managed to sort and catalog all of it.

Emily set the box down and peeled off the tape that crackled with age. Reading labels, she went through a stack of spiral-bound notebooks, clearly notes from more modern researchers: "Maxwell-Beaubien Land Grant, Baca Grande Corporation, Santa Fe Trail …" She set that one aside for her patron who was studying the trail. The others went into a new stack.

Finally, she pulled out a musty, leather-bound album. Her fingers ran over the embossed lettering on its cover, her pulse taking a jump. "Letters of the Graystone Family," she read aloud. Kelly looked up from her file folder.

"Ooh, let's take a look," Kelly suggested, as Emily placed the album on the table and carefully opened it.

The pages revealed letters written in elegant script, some bearing the official Graystone family seal. Flipping through, she noticed the letters seemed to have been gathered and bound in reverse order. The one on top was dated 1935 and was addressed to a Henry Graystone, on a matter pertaining to the family financial situation.

"That was during the Great Depression," Emily said. "At a glance, it appears the Graystones were suffering setbacks. The word bankruptcy appears in here." She flipped the page, sticking with her vow not to get sidetracked by anything not pertaining to Gabriel.

"Look at this one," Kelly said, pointing to a letter dated 1920, about halfway through the volume. It was signed by Nathaniel Graystone, Gabriel's older brother. As Emily began to read it out loud, Kelly leaned in closer, absorbing every word.

"Dearest Mother, I cannot comprehend the foolishness of my younger brother. Why must he insist on breaking his engagement to Clara Maldonado? She is a fine lady and our families have been intertwined for years. It is simply disgraceful that he would turn his back on her and our family's honor."

"Wow," Kelly murmured, her eyes widening in surprise. "Nathaniel didn't seem too pleased with Gabriel's decision."

"*Intertwined?* Isn't that a strange way to refer to an open feud? I wonder if Nathaniel is being truthful with his mother," Emily said. "Gabriel told me his family was opposed to the marriage."

She flipped to another of the letters and continued to read. "Apparently, he's looking out for his own interests. He goes on to say that he fears the consequences of Gabriel's actions will bring shame upon the entire Graystone family. More likely, the breakup might even throw the court's decision about the gold mine in favor of their rivals and Nathaniel portrays himself as the one who will do everything in his power to mend the rift between them and the Maldonados."

"I get the feeling Nathaniel had quite an envious streak," Kelly observed, her brow furrowed in thought. "Maybe he resented his brother for having the freedom to make his own choices, while he was stuck with family obligations."

"Could be that. And it somewhat explains how it ties to the land feud. Let's see if there are more letters from Nathaniel," Emily said, flipping through the album. She stopped at another page, this one dated a day earlier than the previous one she'd read from.

"Dearest Mother," she read, "I can no longer ignore the resentment brewing within me. Gabriel's foolish decision has caused nothing but heartache and strife between our family and the Maldonados. We used to hold our heads high in this town, but now we are whispered about behind closed doors, our name tarnished by my brother's careless actions."

"Sounds like Nathaniel was really bitter about the whole situation."

"Definitely," Emily agreed, feeling a chill run down her spine as she continued to read. "He goes on to say that he believes the Maldonado family will never forgive them for the humiliation they've suffered, and that it's all Gabriel's fault."

"Could Nathaniel's bitterness have exacerbated the feud?" Kelly asked, her voice barely more than a whisper.

"Perhaps," Emily mused, her eyes sad. "It certainly adds a new dimension to the story."

She turned a few more pages, but her thoughts were

churning. "Kel, what if Nathaniel was involved in Gabriel's death?"

"Like he played a part in the feud *and* the murder?" Kelly raised an eyebrow, clearly intrigued by the idea.

"Exactly," Emily said, her fingers tapping the book of letters. "He had motive, didn't he? His resentment towards the Maldonado family, his belief that Gabriel was responsible for everything … Maybe he thought getting rid of Gabriel would end the feud."

"Reading between the lines, I think Nathaniel was jealous of Gabriel. Look at this other letter," Kelly said, pointing to one she had just finished skimming. "He mentions New Mexico politics and the governorship. Then in the very next sentence, there's a not very subtle hint at his perception that Gabriel was their father's favorite son. Jealousy can be a powerful motivator."

"Interesting. Politics and family jealousy. That's a combination that rarely ends well. And remember what we heard about the death of one of the young Maldonado girls."

Kelly looked up and set the old album aside. "Maybe Mom could talk to the Maldonado couple she met? She might learn something more."

Chapter 26

Sam found herself on Zoë's street, making a bakery delivery, so it was not a tricky decision to stop in and say hello. This time, when she pulled into the driveway, the construction trucks were gone. She rapped at the back door, received no answer, and tried the handle. From the kitchen she could hear the sound of a vacuum cleaner running.

"Zoë! Hey, it's Sam!"

The vacuum shut down and Zoë's head appeared in the doorway to the dining room. "Hey, girl, what's up?"

"Just in the neighborhood. What's up with you? Looks like you're in the cleanup phase?"

"Yes, and not a moment too soon. We have guests arriving tomorrow afternoon. The guys put all the furniture in place, and my girls who help with cleaning have made all the beds. I'm just putting away the little stuff, checking everything over so I can start cooking for the guests tomorrow."

"You know, all you have to do is ask and I'll bring whatever you want from the bakery."

"Already on it. I phoned and talked to Jen about thirty minutes ago."

Sam laughed. "I should have known. You're so efficient."

Zoë wheeled the vacuum down the hall and stored it in a closet. "You never said what you've been up to. Can you spare time for a cup of tea?"

"I'd better not right now, Kelly and Emily are at the library digging through old history to find more details about these two families Em is investigating—Graystone and Maldonado. There was a murder in the Graystone family and she's intent on solving it." Sam feigned interest in a small *santo* statue in a niche, so Zoë wouldn't pick up on the fact that she was holding out. If there wasn't time for tea, there certainly wasn't time to go into the whole tale of how Emily was conversing with this ghost and had now traveled back in time.

"Maldonado, you said? Hm. I'd swear I've seen that name someplace, just in the last few days." Zoë turned around, her eyes darting toward the parlor. She headed in that direction and Sam followed.

"Sorry for the mess. This is the last room on my cleaning list." Zoë picked up a stack of books from the coffee table and studied the spines. A slender hardcover volume caught her attention. "I'd forgotten we had this little thing."

Stamped in gold on the front cover were the words: *Nuestra Historia, A Maldonado Family History.* "I'd never heard of them, and I truly don't remember how this book came to be on our shelves." She handed the book to Sam. "Take it, if you'd like."

"Thanks. I'll get it back to you after Emily has a chance to look it over."

"Hey, it's something more appropriate for the research library than here at my house anyway. Tell her to keep it."

Sam tucked the book into her bag and together they walked through the house. Zoë embraced her at the back door and insisted she come back when they could both relax a little and catch up on everything. Back in her van, Sam headed past the Plaza and the bakery, deciding to get the little book to Emily as soon as possible.

Emily looked up from her seat at the worktable, where piles of documents sat surrounding a box labeled Estate Sales.

"Hey, Sam." Emily brushed a strand of hair away from her face, her expression weary.

"You look pooped. Where's your helper?"

"Over here, Mom." Kelly straightened up and pushed at a cardboard box with her foot. "Just trying to put away a few things we've already looked at."

"Brought you a present, from Zoë." Sam pulled the little book from her bag and handed it over.

"Maldonado history? Wow, what a find." Emily immediately dropped the papers she'd been holding and carefully opened the front cover. She smiled as she riffled the pages. "It looks to be a self-published little collection of stories. There's no title page or copyright page, no publisher listed at all. Even the layout seems like something that started on a typewriter. This is amazing."

Sam and Kelly stepped behind her to look over her shoulder.

"Oh wait!" Kelly said. "Back there a page or two, I caught the name Clara Maldonado. That's Gabriel's fiancée, right? I mean, ex. It means the stories at least cover the same time period."

Emily paged backward and found the reference. She began to read aloud. "The children began the day in joy, ended it in tears."

The trio exchanged glances. Emily turned back to the book and began to speed read through the account. "Oh, no. This is the day the little girl died. Her name was Amelia. The Maldonado children were taken on a picnic beside the river. It talks about how they were all having fun, that some other kids were with them, including two of the Graystone boys." She looked up. "Nathaniel and Gabriel, maybe? This doesn't give their names."

She flipped a page and continued. "Sounds like the kids were all hyped up, excited and running around, and little Amelia fell into the river. She drowned before any of the adults could save her."

"Oh no, how tragic," Sam murmured.

"Whoever wrote the story makes no bones about it, they believed the Graystone boys to be responsible. Gabriel was a few years older, it says, and this writer believed he should have been able to save the little girl but that he purposely stood by and watched her die." Emily choked up at this point, her voice raw. "I can't believe that. I know Gabriel. He's a gentle soul."

Kelly put her arm around Emily's shoulders. "It surely was an accident. Kids playing, getting out of sight of the adults. They certainly can't have blamed Gabriel personally."

Tears ran down Emily's face. "But they did. It's spelled out right here."

Chapter 27

Sam gently removed the book from her hands, opening it again to the brief story of the picnic and the tragedy. She read through it as Emily composed herself. It was true. The Graystone family was forever branded in the eyes of the Maldonados. But that was a hundred years ago. Surely today …

"Maybe a visit to the present-day Maldonados would help," Sam suggested. "I can call Annette and see if they've thought of anything since my last visit."

But her phone call went unanswered and when she stopped by the home of Jaime and Annette on her way home, no one answered, despite the fact that two cars sat in the driveway.

They were obviously unwilling to discuss the notorious ancestors.

"Try not to take it personally," Samantha muttered to herself as she walked back to her vehicle.

She phoned Emily and told her what happened. "Jaime must have talked to others in his family. People around here have long memories, especially when it comes to feuds."

"Still," Emily sighed, disappointed by the couple's refusal to help. "You'd think after all these years, they might want the truth to come out."

"Maybe they're afraid of the truth, or maybe they *are* hiding something," Sam told her. "Anyway, I wish you luck in solving this thing."

* * *

Emily turned on more lamps when it became too dark to read in the library. She'd finished going through the box from the estate sale and stashed the documents back inside after making a quick list of names she could use for indexing them. Now, she picked up the slender book Sam had brought over and carried it to her house for an evening of reading.

She made a light snack of crackers and cheese for her dinner and carried the plate to the living room where she settled into a corner of the leather sofa and opened the book. Rereading the chapter about the picnic was no less painful this time, but she was determined to go forward in the story and find out what happened next. No matter how awful it felt to see Gabriel cast in a bad light by the Maldonados, she had to find out if one of them put any admission in writing, something that would lead her to the answers about his murder.

Before she'd made any progress, though, she sensed a presence in the room with her.

"Valerie?"

"It's Gabriel. Forgive my intrusion into your home, but I had the feeling you were thinking of me." He stepped from the hallway into her view. "Have you found my diary? I kept one, but I have no idea what happened to it."

I've been thinking of almost nothing else but you. But she didn't say it aloud. Instead, she held up the book that had occupied her afternoon and told him what she'd read.

His handsome face reflected sadness. "Ah, that day at the river. It was one of the worst in my young life. I was ten. My brothers were there, as well, but being twelve, thirteen, and fourteen they kept to themselves rather than playing silly games with us. Clara and one of her sisters were there. Amelia was a cousin of theirs, and only four years old. She wanted to tag along. The girls indulged her. I found myself somewhat alone, not so much interested in the games the girls played, not accepted by the older boys. I was standing by the river's edge, attempting to skip stones. The girls were in the clearing behind me, laughing and shrieking."

He began to pace in front of her.

"I didn't realize at first when the shrieks of the girls turned into screams. I was simply ignoring their game, I thought. It took a full minute or two for me to realize Amelia was in the water and they were screaming for help. By the time I saw the little girl some of the adults had arrived as well. Someone jumped in and pulled her out, but it was too late."

"What happened next? I mean, to you?"

He shook his head slowly side to side. "My father grabbed me and my mother came and picked me up. All of Clara's family were gathered around Amelia on the ground."

His expression turned wistful. "I can only imagine that I was a bit heavy for my mother to keep holding me in her arms, but she did. After that, I don't know. I suppose we went home. The picnic and the fun day were over."

"Do you know what the Maldonado family said about it? Later?"

He shook his head, so she read from the book.

"The youngest Graystone boy, Gabriel, was alone with Amelia beside the river. He had a stone in his hand. What was said between them, he never revealed. All we knew was that our baby was dead and he was the only one to see it happen. His parents have sheltered him, but that boy, and his entire family, will burn in hell."

"What!" Gabriel's ghostly face turned even more gaunt, gray with shock.

Emily felt tears overflow her eyes as she looked at him.

"No! That is not at all what happened. They imply—" His face reddened and he clenched his fists. "A stone in my hand? A small one, flat and made for skipping across the water. I never—"

He paced the length of the carpet again and turned to her. "Emily, you don't believe that I could—I mean, a ten-year-old child. What motive could I have had? None! I had no reason to harm that little girl. She was Clara's cousin! I would have never hurt her."

"I know. I believe you." As soon as she spoke the words, his image vanished.

But Emily had to admit to herself that she could also see why the Maldonados had a longstanding hatred of Gabriel Graystone.

Chapter 28

The sharp scent of roasted green chile floated on the air, drawing Sam toward the twice-weekly farmer's market. She walked the two blocks from Sweet's Sweets, hoping to connect with the merchant who sold the cinnamon and nutmeg she preferred. Although a little on the pricey side, the spices were far superior to what her mother would have termed 'store bought.'

And there she was ... the little woman with wavy dark hair and a sparkle in her smile. She was in the midst of being berated by an elderly man who seemed to be taking exception to the prices. "I'm sorry, sir, everything has gotten more expensive lately and I can't control what my suppliers charge." The item under debate looked like a container of some kind, a small urn.

The man with the slicked-back gray hair gave her an

ugly scowl and walked away, grumbling.

The vendor greeted Sam with a smile and reached under her table. "I'm glad you told me you were running low on these last week. I don't always bring everything with me."

Sam chose the spices she wanted, paid, and visited with the lady until another customer walked up. Across the way, next to the man who was operating the propane-fired chile roaster, she spotted Emily. She walked over to join her.

"Hey, how's it going?"

Emily visibly jumped. "Oh! Sam. Sorry."

"What? Something wrong?"

Em shook her head, her blond hair swinging. "I don't know. Well, not really. But I'm not sure." She glanced nervously over her shoulder.

"Okay, *something* is wrong. What's going on?" Sam took her friend's elbow and steered her toward a shady spot away from the crowd.

Emily stood with her back to the tree. "I can't shake the feeling that I'm being watched, like I'm seeing shadowy figures lurking in doorways or alleys, and it's as if someone's breathing on me." She raised a hand and rubbed her neck nervously.

"Are you okay?" Sam asked.

"I don't know," Emily admitted, rubbing her arms as a shiver ran through her. "I can't help but feel like we're being followed."

"All of us? By whom?"

Emily shook her head and forced a smile. "Maybe it's just my imagination."

Sam wasn't convinced. "You have a good sense about things like this, so I think we should be extra cautious. If we're on the right track with our case, there might be people who don't want us to uncover the truth." She reminded Emily of the snubbing she'd received when she tried to visit with Annette Maldonado for a second time.

"I know, it seems so strange. But Gabriel feels it too. He visited me again last evening as I was going through that little book of Maldonado history. He was quite upset to learn that the family suspected him in the death of that little girl. It was heartbreaking to watch his reaction."

Sam nodded in sympathy. "I do hope we can figure—" Her phone vibrated in her pocket, interrupting. She pulled it out and looked at the number.

"It's Evan Richards," she told Emily, as she tapped to answer the call.

"Sam, good news," he said. "I've got those blueprints for you. And a key."

Sam gave Emily a thumbs-up and thanked Evan. "I'm at the farmer's market right now, so I'll just walk on over to your office if that's okay."

"I'll be here."

She ended the call. "We can get into Graystone Manor," she said with a grin.

"Yay! I really hope we can find something useful. If nothing else, I'd love to see the place where Gabriel grew up."

"Before we rush over there, I want to study the plans and put together some ideas of what we're looking for," Sam said.

"When should we do this?" Emily asked. "I've got a researcher coming by the library in about fifteen minutes, so I ought to get back."

"And I didn't actually plan to be away from the bakery quite this long either," Sam admitted. "I'll get the blueprints from Evan, and then we can touch base a little later. I should have some free time this afternoon."

"And check with Kelly, too. I'm sure she'd want to be in on this."

Sam chuckled. "No doubt. Okay, that's our plan."

She watched Emily head south, back toward home, and couldn't help but notice that her friend looked around in all directions and over her shoulder. She was obviously still worried.

Sam walked through the farmer's market lot and crossed Camino de la Placita. Evan's office was only a couple of blocks north and east. He met her at the back entrance, in the lot where the cruisers parked.

"Thought I'd save you having to negotiate the lobby," he said, holding out a rolled-up set of plans, then dropping a large old-fashioned key into her hand. "I'll need to return those when you're done. The plans came from County Zoning, and the key was with a Realtor who is currently trying to sell the place. I made her think you were a potential buyer, so play along with that if the subject comes up."

"I can assure you I'm not in the market for a mansion," Sam said with a wry grin, "but thanks for the heads-up."

It was close to four p.m. before Sam found a moment to take an extra breath and make phone calls. Kelly had just walked in the door after picking up Scott at the airport. Seemed his book tour had brought him as close to home as Phoenix and he'd hopped a quick Southwest flight to spend a couple of days with his girls before heading out for Los Angeles.

"Oh, I absolutely do want to go along!" Kelly said when Sam told her what was going on, and that she and Emily planned to go out to the Graystone mansion.

"Can you be at Emily's place in fifteen minutes? Bring the book of runes and your box," Sam advised. "We have no idea what we'll encounter out there."

They had the blueprints spread out on Emily's worktable in the library when Kelly arrived. Emily was tracing her finger over the layout of the old house.

"Look at this," Samantha whispered, pointing to a small notation on the edge of the map. "There's something handwritten here—hidden passage."

"A secret passage?" Emily's heart raced even faster. "Could it possibly be connected to the rest of the tunnel system?"

Sam chewed at her lower lip. "I don't see how. The mansion is quite a lot farther from the center of town."

"Still, there are a lot of unexplainable things down there, and remember what Iris Maxwell told us," Emily reminded.

"Let's go check it out," Kelly suggested, her eyes gleaming with excitement.

"Can I ask … and I apologize if I'm sounding paranoid," Emily said, "But did either of you notice someone watching you as you came here? We need to make sure we're not being followed."

"Good idea," Samantha agreed. "We'll have to be smart about this. Maybe we should take more than one vehicle and drive there by different routes."

Emily took a deep breath. "Yes, I would definitely feel better about that."

Chapter 29

As she approached the three-story mansion, Emily shivered. If there was a word for unease combined with anticipation, that's what she felt. The Victorian manor house sat on a dirt road on the south side of town, high on a small rise, with a clear view of the western horizon. The home's name was fitting—made entirely of gray stone, with a portico in front, curved windows, and two turrets. Numerous chimneys rose from the steeply peaked roof. None of the building materials were native to northern New Mexico, so the place must have cost a fortune to build. Completely different from the prevalent adobe and occasional wooden structures in town, this one stood out.

Ivy had once covered the northern turret wall, another luxury in the high desert climate. One of the owners along the way had installed a large lawn, and stone borders framed what were probably abundant flowerbeds, but all of that had long since died away. A low wall edged the front of the property, speaking of a time when appearances were more important than the safety of high walls and alarms, unlike the present when yards were, by necessity, planted with drought tolerant plants and cost was nearly always a factor.

Emily squinted in the bright afternoon light, imagining the place in its excessive glory years, imagining Gabriel growing up here as a young boy. The aesthetics of the house would have appealed to the artist in him. She'd no sooner relaxed into that feeling than the uneasiness shadowed her again.

She shook off the feeling, reminding herself that she'd been diligent while driving here and had spotted no one tailing her. Sam pulled in behind Emily's Jeep, less than two minutes later, and Kelly was close behind.

"Stay near," Emily instructed, as they slipped through the overgrown garden and made their way toward the house. "We don't know what we're walking into."

"I've got an idea," Kelly said, pulling the carved wooden box from her bag. "I hope to pick up on paranormal activity. If there's something spooky going on, this should let us know." In her hands, the box began to glow, the wood becoming warmer. She took a deep breath.

Nothing appeared right away. The quiet was pervasive, almost a presence itself. The sun was low in the clear sky, and Sam reminded them that they probably had less than two hours until dark.

Emily seemed focused on the sights and sounds around them, but no one detected another presence. "Perfect," Emily said, feeling a little more reassured. "Let's go inside."

They stepped under the portico and walked up to the

ornate front entry. Sam pulled the large key from her pocket and the trio entered the huge home. The heavy wooden door opened into a wide foyer with black and white marble flooring, probably original, and a curved staircase on their right led to the second story.

According to the plans, that was where the bedrooms were located. The ground floor was originally a typical Victorian layout, with a formal parlor, a large dining room, a library, and study, with a big kitchen and butler's pantry at the back of the house. But all that had changed. The wealthy tech guy had gone with a completely modern vibe, pure white walls, metal tubing for stair railings, and an open floor plan that echoed obnoxiously with their every footstep.

"So disappointing. I'd hoped it would look like it did in Gabriel's day," Emily murmured. "Too bad all the remodeling and various uses over the years changed it so drastically."

Kelly agreed. "It would be nice if the next buyer were to go back and restore it to the period, but I doubt that will happen."

Sam spoke up. "While we have lots of light, let's go upstairs and take a peek. We can explore the basement and anything subterranean by flashlight anytime."

Emily led the way to what she believed, from the original plans, must have been Gabriel's bedroom. Standing in the middle of it, she closed her eyes and concentrated on picking up some kind of vibration that would relate to him. But, sadly, nothing came to her. A hundred years of other occupants had erased his spirit from the place.

"Sorry, Gabriel," she whispered as she left the room.

Sam and Kelly had peeked into each of the other

bedrooms and the bathrooms, including those in what was originally the attic and probably servants quarters. "Everything has been so modernized it doesn't even seem like a true Victorian anymore," Sam said. "For the record, I must say that I love what you and Scott have done with yours, the way you kept Eliza Nalespar's essence in every room."

"Well, except that Scott insisted on a big-screen TV," Kelly said with a laugh that lightened the mood.

Emily asked Sam to unroll the blueprints again. "Let's take a look and see if we can find the way to that secret passage."

A few minutes later they were descending stone steps to the basement. Although the space had long since been cleared of any furnishings or other historical memorabilia, their lights did reveal a small doorway. Opening it, they discovered only a closet.

"Storage." Emily looked with disgust at the plain wooden shelving.

Sam shone her flashlight again at the plans. "There could still be something here. I'm thinking it's beyond this closet. Let's see if we can remove the shelves."

Luck was with them, as the shelves rested on wooden braces along the sides and back, and no one had bothered to nail them down. Sam lifted each shelf and handed it off to the others. With her heavy flashlight, she began tapping the back wall. It seemed solid. Same with the side wall on the right. But the side wall on the left echoed with another sound.

"It's hollow behind there," Emily said, practically holding her breath as Sam tapped it again. She bumped the baseboard with the toe of her sneaker, testing it for solidity. And that's when something gave way.

The baseboard fell forward, revealing a dull metal piece. When Sam knelt and touched that, it proved to be a spring mechanism. The entire left wall swung inward with a screech that chilled the bones.

Chapter 30

Okay, I am officially a little freaked out," Emily admitted. "I really wasn't sure anything would be here."

They crowded into the closet and shined all three of their flashlights around the newfound opening. This was the one area of the house that didn't appear to have been touched in modern times. The walls were concrete and a narrow set of stone steps led downward. Strands of cobwebs laced across the passage.

"Ew, I'm not touching those," Kelly said.

Sam gave her daughter a look. "Seriously. I'll do it." She removed her jacket and waved it through the air, breaking a path through the webs. "Luckily, this is washable."

The others followed her until they reached a flat, tiled floor. They were in a small room, maybe ten feet on each side.

"Okay, that's a little disappointing," Emily said. "This is it?"

Sam aimed her light around a corner and discovered another opening. "Looks like this leads into a bigger space."

Emily followed as Sam lit the way, with Kelly trailing behind.

"Mommm … look at this," Kelly called out.

They turned to see that the wooden box's soft, eerie glow had deepened. "Something's definitely here with us," Kelly whispered, her voice trembling.

"Told you someone's been watching us." Despite trying to take a light approach, Emily's voice sounded a little shaky.

"I'm going with it being the spirit of Gabriel," Kelly said. "We want this to be a friendly entity."

Sam interrupted their little wisecracks. "Look. Right there."

She aimed her flash at a corner of the larger chamber, revealing stacks of trunks and wooden boxes. Queen Anne tables and Tiffany lamps sat neatly together. A dressmaker's form, a globe of the world, some quaint Christmas decorations—all were coated in a century's worth of dust, but all were beautifully preserved in the arid climate.

Emily rushed to investigate the trove, opening one of the trunks immediately. "These belonged to the Graystones, things they either forgot or were unable to take with them when they moved away." She pulled out a stack of neatly folded silk scarves and a man's sweater which, unfortunately, moths had already discovered. Beneath them were packets of letters tied with ribbon.

"The return address on this one shows it came from Augustine Maldonado. Oh my gosh." She carefully lifted the flap and pulled out a single sheet of paper. "Guys, listen to this," Emily said, her voice barely audible. "It's written to Nathaniel Graystone, and it details plans to meet at the Plaza. This was right before Gabriel was killed. They were plotting something together."

"Could it be that they were *both* involved in Gabriel's death?"

"Only one way to find out," Emily replied, her eyes shining. "We need to keep digging."

They propped their flashlights to illuminate the area and set to work. Within an hour they had accumulated a sizeable stack of letters and documents.

"What are we going to do with all this?" Kelly asked.

"None of it belongs to us—or to anyone living today, that we know of," Sam said. "I think the appropriate place for it would be the Morton Library, Em. Your family has done such an amazing job of preserving the history of Taos, and this is definitely part of that."

Emily started to pick up the letters.

"But," Sam continued, "it doesn't belong to us, and we'd better do this right. Whoever owns the house is technically the owner of the contents."

"Evan told me no one owns the house. The rich guy went bankrupt and the place has been tied up in foreclosure."

Sam thought for a minute. "I used to break into houses that were in this very situation. I was hired to clear them out so they could be sold."

"And?"

"I could do anything I wanted with the contents, but … that was because I had permission from the mortgage holder. I have no idea who that would be, in this case."

Emily hugged a packet of letters to her chest. "I hate

to let Gabriel's family history slip away, to be decided by a banker somewhere." Her voice sounded tight.

"How about this?" Sam suggested. "Let's pack up the documentation—letters, diaries, books, and whatever. We'll take those to your library. We'll let both the real estate agent and the sheriff know where they are."

"Agreed," Emily said. "Hopefully, it will get sorted out so the documents can remain with the library, available to anyone who needs them for their research work." She set to work, filling one of the wooden crates with the important items.

Thirty minutes later, after carrying the crate upstairs and re-concealing the door to the secret room, the three of them stood outside the mansion.

"Ugh, I can't believe how much dust we inhaled." Kelly sneezed and wiped at her reddened nose. "Did you notice that the box went dark and cool once we discovered the hidden room? It's as if it was telling us there was more to the situation, leading us to discover what we did. It was definitely worth it."

"Agreed," Samantha said, leading the way to their vehicles. "I never thought we'd find such damning evidence against Nathaniel Graystone."

"Nor did I," Kelly added, her eyes clouded with worry. "Think of it. The letters between Nathaniel and Augustine, the secret meeting… It's like something straight out of a novel."

"Except this is real life, and we're dealing with a dangerous feud that goes back more than a century," Emily reminded them, her voice firm.

"Right," Kelly agreed. "So, what's our next move?"

"First, we need to figure out if the Maldonados Sam

met are descendants of Augustine or Antonio," Emily replied, her thoughts racing. "We should also look into the Graystones' side of the story. Where did they go when they left Taos, why does it seem they left in a huge hurry, and are any of their descendants still around? Who knows what else we might uncover?"

"Good idea," Samantha said. "Maybe we can find something more among those records and newspapers from the 1920s that will tell us."

"Exactly," Emily added. "And let's keep this quiet for now. We don't want to take the chance that someone out there still cares to keep this feud going."

"Got it," Kelly whispered, her eyes wide. "Mum's the word."

"All right, let's wrap it up for today," Emily decided. "We'll meet again tomorrow morning at Sweet's Sweets. I have a feeling we're getting a lot closer."

Samantha and Kelly nodded in agreement. The sun had set long ago, and as they drove into the darkness it felt as though the shadows of the past were following closely behind.

* * *

Beau glanced sideways at Sam's balled-up jacket when she walked in the house.

"Cobwebs. Don't ask."

"Okay …"

"All right, you can ask, but let me toss this in the washer and have a shower first." She proceeded up the stairs and came down twenty minutes later feeling like a new person.

"We got the key to the old Graystone mansion and

went exploring," she said, gratefully accepting the bowl of soup he'd dished up for her. "Lots of dust, lots of spider webs, and *lots* of old papers and stuff. I don't envy Emily having to read through and document it all, but that's her thing. I tell you, the girl loves it that she gets to take over her grandfather's work. Me, I'd rather decorate cakes any day."

"So, how's the case going?" he asked, reaching for a saltine and breaking it up in his own soup.

Sam filled him in. "Gabriel was murdered in 1920, and all fingers pointed to a man named Tomas Ramos, supposedly hired by Clara Maldonado's two brothers. I've met some present-day Maldonados, but they seem to be giving me the cold shoulder after initially seeming pretty friendly. I'm not sure what's up with that."

Beau seemed thoughtful. "There's still at least one Ramos here in town. They have a little business called Ramos Imports. Brings in stuff from Mexico—pottery, blankets, silver jewelry and such. It's a small shop out by the turnoff to the Martinez Hacienda. We always kind of suspected they were running something shady on the side because we couldn't imagine anyone making a living from the junk they sell there. But there was never any real proof. Maybe there's a connection with the Ramos from the past?"

Sam smiled. "We'd better refer to the *junk* as arts and crafts, but yeah, maybe I'll just plan to pay Ramos Imports a visit in the morning. Hopefully I can learn some information about Tomas that could help us."

Chapter 31

The following morning, Sam stepped into the dimly lit Ramos Imports. The scent of aged wood and musty fabrics filled the air as she wandered the crowded aisles of the shop, browsing shelves loaded with pottery, glassware, blankets, placemats, shawls, and t-shirts with tacky artwork and strange slogans. Finally, she approached an elderly man behind the counter.

"Good morning," Samantha greeted, setting a ceramic spoon holder on the counter and pulling out her wallet. "I'm doing some historical research for the Morton Library here in town, and we've come across the name Tomas Ramos, from back in the 1920s. The librarian thought you might be related?"

A flicker of recognition crossed his face, a millisecond before his smile faded. "Why you are asking?"

"As I said, we came across his name in the papers of someone else who lived in town at that time, a Gabriel Graystone. I got the impression he and Tomas were good friends. Would you happen to have any old records or papers that may have belonged to him? We'd merely like to borrow them, and I'd bring them back."

Something in the old man's expression shut down. He glanced at the spoon holder. "Three dollars."

"But—can you tell me anything at all about Tomas? Maybe you remember him from when you were a kid or something?"

He turned away, making a fuss over wrapping the ceramic item in newspaper and stuffing it into a small shopping bag. "Three dollars."

Sam pulled three singles from her wallet and held them slightly out of his reach. "Anything you remember could be helpful."

He shifted the bagged item so it was out of her reach.

Really, we're going to play this game? She set the money on the counter and dropped her wallet back into her bag. When she looked up again, the shopping bag was right there, and the man had become busy with something in a display case.

"Well, thanks so much for your time," she called as she walked out.

She started her truck and headed for the center of town. She'd asked Sheriff Richards to dig around a little and see if law enforcement records still existed for the time when Ramos was a suspect in Gabriel's death, something that went beyond what the newspaper had covered. She was hoping that's what he'd found, based on the text she received during breakfast, asking her to stop by. The morning traffic on Paseo was light, and she arrived at the department parking lot in less than fifteen minutes.

The new desk officer was apparently starting to recognize her, because she sent Sam on back to the squad room. Evan walked in, a dark brown folder tucked under his arm.

"Hey, Sam," he greeted. "I did some digging after you said you were looking into the old Ramos case. Here's what I found in the case files. It's Tomas's written statement to the sheriff." He handed Samantha a sheet of what looked like old notebook paper.

"Thanks, Evan," she said, looking at the page and reading aloud: "I swear, I never touched Gabriel Graystone. I was hired to take care of him, but when the time came, I couldn't do it. He was my friend. My conscience wouldn't allow it." She looked up. "Do you think he was telling the truth?"

Evan shrugged. "Standard procedure would be to advise the suspect that they are writing out their statement under oath. I don't know what was done back then."

"Based on this, they ruled out Tomas as the murderer? Wouldn't they have checked for an alibi?"

"Yeah, but in my opinion that was pretty inconclusive. Ramos said he was home, helping his father with something. The parents verified that."

"Naturally. So Ramos was released."

"Looks that way. There's not much else in the file to help us figure out who actually killed Gabriel."

"That's not a very thick folder," Sam said.

"They didn't create the massive case files we see today. A hundred years ago, law enforcement was a simpler thing. They found the guilty party and hung 'em." He held up a hand. "I'm joking. But the tricky burden-of-proof scenarios that we routinely face today … it just wasn't like that." He set the folder aside. "It appears they asked questions, followed leads, and then ran out of leads. That happens. Even now, not every case gets solved."

Sam chafed in frustration.

"Hey, I welcome your help. If you ladies can find a valid suspect and that person is still around, I'll follow up with it. This is technically still an open case."

"Yeah, right," she said with a laugh. "We've had a hard time finding anyone in the present time who knows anything at all. I made contact with a couple of the Maldonados, but they shut me down. Now this Ramos guy with the import shop did the same. I swear, when I mentioned Gabriel Graystone's name, the man completely clammed up."

"Oh! That reminds me," Evan said, turning toward his office and beckoning her to follow. "I did find some historical data about the Graystone family."

He sat at his desk and brought his computer screen to life. Sam walked around so she could look over his shoulder.

"These are records from the state legislature, data from the 1920s to the 1940s. There was a Graystone … a Nathaniel … who ran for state senator and held office. He became the senator from Santa Fe County."

"Hm. Interesting. So that would mean the Graystone family moved to Santa Fe at some point. The timeframe you're showing here fits with what we've learned in connection with the Graystone mansion. They left Taos after the tragedy and never lived in this town again."

"But at least some of them were close enough—Santa Fe."

"And Nathaniel went into politics. I believe one of

the documents we came across indicated the patriarch had hoped Gabriel would run for governor. Looks like Nathaniel filled his shoes."

"Although he never got elected as governor."

"Evan, is there a way to print this page, or at least take a screenshot? I'd like to share the information, dates, etcetera with Emily."

"No problem." He tapped a few keys then stood up.

Sam followed him to the printer in the squad room, where he retrieved the page. She thanked him and promised to get out of his hair. He wished her luck in the search, but she got the feeling he was only humoring her. If his days were anything like Beau's when he held this job, there was a never-ending flow of calls to handle and an old case, especially one that was impossible to prosecute, was miniscule on the priority list.

She said goodbye to the desk officer and pushed through the doors to the parking lot. She'd unlocked her truck and climbed into the driver's seat when she spotted a uniformed deputy walking toward her. She didn't recognize him.

"I was in the squad room and overheard what you and Sheriff Richards were talking about," he said. "He's mentioned this old case to all of us, mostly just in passing. Anyway, this was given to me." He held up a small book. "My cousin is Sophie Garcia. She's a caregiver for the elderly, and she asked if I could find you and pass this along. She thought it might be of interest."

Sam felt her brow furrow as he handed her the book, which looked like just one more in the long series of journals and leatherbound books she'd been seeing in recent days. "Um, okay."

The deputy turned away and was halfway back to the door when she looked up again. Her phone pinged with a text from Becky at the bakery, a reminder that there was a birthday cake to deliver this morning. She started her truck and headed for Sweet's Sweets.

The hours flew, and five p.m. came around before Sam had a clue. Beau called with a reminder that they'd made dinner plans with friends, and asking whether she wanted to come home first or meet him at the restaurant at six.

Sam looked down at her sugar-dusted black slacks and smudged baker's jacket. "I'd better come home for a quick shower. I'm leaving now."

Out in her truck she spotted the little book the deputy had handed her earlier in the day. Ugh, one more thing. But it would be a quick stop to drop it off to Emily. The library was only a couple of blocks from her shop, and she could then take the back route home rather than getting tangled in the Plaza traffic.

Chapter 32

Emily heard a vehicle pull into the library parking space. She wasn't expecting anyone and felt tempted to turn off the light. Her head was pounding after sorting and reading the stacks of documents they'd recovered from Graystone Manor yesterday. But when she glanced up, she saw the visitor was Sam, still dressed in her bakery attire. She rushed to open the front door.

"Hey, Em, I can't stay," Sam said. "I'm already running late for some evening plans with Beau. But I thought you might want this right away." She held out a small leatherbound book.

Emily turned it over in her hands. Embossed on the front cover, small and unobtrusive, were two letters: G.G.

"What—? Where did you—"

"It was handed over to me by one of Evan's deputies,"

Sam called out as she dashed back to her truck.

Her mind reeling, Emily watched her friend back out and drive away. Gabriel had said something about his own diary, wondering if Emily had come across it. And now it appeared to be here, right in her hands. Talk about the universe delivering! The moment she had the thought, she backtracked. There was no way to know whether the diary would include any new information or merely more of what she'd already been reading in other Graystone family documents.

She walked back into the library, hugging the small book to her chest as she locked up. She took a few minutes to neaten her desk and turn out the lights, then carried Gabriel's diary to her house, where she searched the medicine cabinet for some desperately needed aspirin.

Once the headache began to subside, she made a ham sandwich, grabbed an apple, and decided to call it dinner. Sitting at the kitchen table, she opened the diary, debating whether to read it all, from the beginning, or to find out what his final days had brought.

"The latter," she told herself. "Let's just cut to the chase."

She began carefully turning the fragile pages until she came to blank ones in the final quarter of the book. There was an entry dated just days before his death.

I have never felt such a mixture of love and fear in my life. Clara's love consumes me, yet I am terrified of what might happen if my secret were ever to be discovered. And now, Iris has confessed her feelings for me as well. I cannot bear the thought of hurting either of them, but my heart belongs to only one.

Iris? Was he writing about Iris Maxwell? Emily pushed her plate aside and stood up, pacing the kitchen floor. And why didn't he say which one his heart belonged to?

"Gabriel! Can you hear me? Please come here." Her shouts turned to pleas. "Gabriel? Where are you …?"

She wanted to scream to the four walls but her voice failed her. She thought of their meetings, of his gentle voice and radiant smile. She could easily see how two women could fall in love with him.

I could fall for him.

She stopped in her tracks. "No, I could not," she sternly lectured herself. "He's a ghost, for heaven's sake! Talk about an unavailable male."

She picked up her plate and dumped the scraps in the trash. Her stomach was churning and her mind was roiling.

This news could change everything. She needed to talk it out with somebody, and since Gabriel was apparently hiding out—from her?—she thought of Sam and Kelly. She flung herself down on the living room sofa and picked up her phone. Sam had said something about plans with Beau. She couldn't interrupt date night. She dialed Kelly instead.

"There's a new twist in Gabriel's story," she began. "I need another opinion. Can I come over?"

Kelly paused. "Sure. Can we plan on sometime after eight? By then Scott will be reading Ana her bedtime story, and we can have some uninterrupted time."

Two hours dragged by, during which Emily found herself getting into the rocky road ice cream. She picked up Gabriel's diary again and began reading earlier entries. The clues were there, but in the true fashion of a clueless man, Gabriel hadn't figured out Iris's true feelings for him until it was too late. He was caught up in clandestine encounters and lies to both his family and Clara's, before he could figure out what his own true feelings were. She found herself reading between the lines to see if the Maldonado brothers were on to him, but if they were Gabriel had not realized it or put it in writing.

She tilted her head back, her mind buzzing, and tried calling out to him again. This would be so much easier if he were here and could tell her what was going on.

The timer on her phone beeped to remind her it was time to leave for Kelly's house. She put on a light jacket and gathered her purse and the diary before walking out to her Jeep. Ten minutes later, she was pulling up outside the classic Victorian where Sam had once run her chocolates business. Later, Kelly and Scott had turned it back to a home. Lights glowed from the windows, bringing back memories of holiday meals where Emily had been included. She parked and walked up to the front door; she could see Kelly's shadow behind the beveled glass insert.

"Hey, girl," Kelly greeted with a smile. "Wow. You seriously look like you could use a glass of wine."

Chapter 33

Emily followed Kelly into her large kitchen and propped a hip against the counter as Kelly poured two glasses of wine.

"Okay, you've got me hooked," Kelly said as they clinked glasses. "You said there's a new twist?"

Emily held up her wine glass. "Gabriel's diary."

"Was it among those things we found at the mansion?"

"Actually, no. This came somewhat round about. Your mom said a deputy at the sheriff's office had it. Sam didn't realize what it was until she handed it off to me and I noticed the initials." She held up the leatherbound book and pointed to the cover.

Kelly squinted at the small letters. "This is Gabriel's diary?"

Emily nodded.

"And so … what's the twist? Don't hold out on me."

"Gabriel was apparently involved with Iris Maxwell at the same time he was engaged to Clara Maldonado."

"Whoa, Gabriel, two women on the string at once! Um, he's not here with you, is he?" Emily shook her head and Kelly took a swig of her wine. "Did he … Did you get a chance to ask him about that?"

Emily glanced toward the back staircase. "Maybe we should go over this up in your private little domain."

"Good idea. Ana should almost be asleep by now, but it sounds like we want to keep this a secret." Kelly led the way to the third floor.

She unlocked the attic door, switched on a lamp, and cleared a space on the window seat cushion. From the second floor, they could hear Scott telling Ana to close her eyes and go to sleep, then his footsteps crossed to his office in the turret. She gently closed the door.

Emily set her wine on a small side table and opened the diary to the page with Gabriel's admission on it. "Read it for yourself."

She sipped her wine while Kelly read.

"It's hard to tell, by what he says here, if this was a full-on affair with Iris or more like her telling him of her feelings," Kelly said.

"But he wouldn't have been so torn unless he somewhat reciprocated that, would he? I mean, this is his private diary. He's not saying he brushed Iris off and told her to go away."

"True." Kelly paused in thought for a minute. "I wonder if we could learn anything from the book of runes."

She stood up and went to the cupboard where she kept the mystical artifact. Resuming her seat next to Emily and holding the book on her lap, she let it fall open naturally to a random page. It was filled with large text, but the rune-like figures were unreadable.

"Hold on," Kelly said.

She left the book with Emily and went back to the cupboard, where she pulled out the carved box and held it close to her body. Within a couple minutes, the wood began to warm and glow. She rubbed her hands over its lumpy surface and concentrated, her eyes closed.

"Let's try this again." She set the box down on her worktable and went back to the book.

This time when Kelly looked at the runes, they appeared to her in English. "Can you read them, Em?"

Emily shook her head.

"Okay, that's all right. What I'm seeing is this: ***The handsome one faces danger. He must watch out for a pair.***"

"That's it?" Emily stared at the page as the runes began to fade away. "A pair of what?"

Kelly's mouth twisted in a little grimace. "It goes this way sometimes. The book presents a puzzle or conundrum."

"Well, we know that there are two Maldonado brothers, and the rumor was they had something to do with Gabriel's death."

"But the sheriff at the time believed their alibis and they were cleared."

"And so now we know there were two women in his life. That's a different pair." Emily's eyes settled on the page again, and she watched in amazement as a different set of characters began to emerge. "What's it saying now?"

Kelly waited until the letters became clear. "***Beware, a confrontation.***"

"Yeah, well, he died. I'd say that was a pretty bad

confrontation." Emily slugged back the last of her wine. "Is there anything more, something to identify the killer?"

But the message faded and nothing more appeared. The two women exchanged a look. "Okay, let's take a look at this logically," Kelly said. "We've heard that Augustine and Antonio Maldonado were known for their ruthlessness in business. Seems they would be the same in personal matters, as well."

"Maybe," Emily mused, her brow furrowing in thought. "They could have seen the love triangle as a threat to their family's reputation."

"Or maybe they were just trying to protect their sister Clara," Kelly suggested. "If either of them found out about Gabriel's entanglement with Iris, they might have sought revenge."

"Either way," Emily concluded, "we can't ignore the possibility that they were involved in the crime and just managed to come up with fake alibis. We can't assume anything at this point."

"True." Kelly returned the book of runes to its place in the cupboard. "May I see the diary again?"

Emily handed over the old book and Kelly gently flipped through the yellowed pages. "Looks like Gabriel kept this journal for several years. It starts out with tales of his being in school, and most of the people he mentions are his immediate family." She paged further in. "The first mention of Clara comes about a year before he died. He seems stunned that their childhood friendship is turning into something more serious."

"Oh my gosh, Gabriel's got a crush!" Emily teased, peering at the words Kelly was pointing to.

"It does sound like he loved her," Kelly admitted.

She started to turn another page when the book slipped in her grasp. A folded piece of paper drifted to the floor.

Emily bent down and picked it up and unfolded it to reveal a sheet of pink stationery, inked in a delicate, looping script. She could almost detect a faint scent of lilacs. She scanned to the bottom of the page.

"It's a letter to Gabriel. Listen to this," Emily murmured, her voice barely audible. "Iris writes, 'My heart is torn in two. I know you love me with a passion that consumes us both, but your loyalty to Clara has tethered you to her like a chain. We meet in secret, our stolen moments filled with equal parts guilt and ecstasy. I can't help but wonder if it will all come crashing down, leaving our broken hearts in its wake.'"

Emily and Kelly exchanged glances, their eyes wide with shock at the confession. This seemed far deeper than Gabriel had admitted.

"Keep reading," Kelly urged.

"Here, she writes about a confrontation between Gabriel and Clara," Emily continued, her finger tracing the lines of text. "'When Clara confronted us on the street today, her accusations of you breaking her heart, shattering her dreams for a future together—in that moment, I saw the truth. My darling, you never intended to marry me. You have been trapped between two desires, unable to choose between us. And yet, I still love you with every fiber of my being. I always will.'"

"Oh boy." Kelly's hand covered her mouth. "So, Clara knew about the affair all along …"

"Here's a PS," Emily said softly. "'I heard whispers in town today – whispers of revenge. Be careful of the Maldonado brothers, my love. Perhaps our love has doomed us all, leaving a trail of broken hearts and shattered lives.'" Emily swallowed hard, her eyes shining with emotion. "That's it. That's where it ends."

Kelly cleared her throat. "Well, it's a bit flowery in the language," she said with a shaky laugh. "But you can tell Iris genuinely cared for Gabriel's safety, with her warning about Clara's brothers."

"And … If Augustine and Antonio were seeking revenge for Clara … what if they didn't know about Iris? How does that complicate the whole situation?"

Emily's fingers tapped nervously on the diary, her thoughts racing. It was a lot of new information to process.

"Okay, let me see if I've got this straight," Kelly said, leaning against the worktable. "Clara was engaged to Gabriel, but he refused to marry her … because he was secretly in love with Iris? Really?"

"I don't know …" Emily said, chewing at a cuticle. "Gabriel's words make it sound like he genuinely loved Clara. But if that's the case, what was he doing meeting in secret with Iris? I think the next time I see him, I want to throttle the man."

"And then," Kelly inserted, "If Tomas Ramos couldn't go through with the hit, and the Maldonado brothers didn't know about Iris … who actually killed Gabriel?"

"Maybe someone else had a motive?" Emily suggested, her voice hesitant. "Someone we haven't considered yet? There may be much more to the story than what's in the diary."

"There has to be something we're missing."

"Right," Emily agreed, her heart pounding. "So, maybe it's back to the library and the things we found at Graystone Manor?"

"Do you want me to come with you?"

"Oh, no. It's late and we're tired. Let's plan on getting together in the morning." Emily stifled a yawn and closed the diary, tucking it into her purse.

She peeked into Scott's study on the way downstairs, saying goodnight and making a polite inquiry about his continuing book tour.

"First thing in the morning," he said. "I'm heading south for a signing in Albuquerque then catching a flight to L.A. Finishing up the west coast in the coming week, and then it's home to begin working on the next book. People are already asking about it."

She gave him a smile and a thumbs-up, and Kelly walked her out to her Jeep. The open countryside around the Victorian was quiet, with only the chittering of night insects in the nearby trees. The girls hugged and said goodnight.

Emily took the back roads and arrived home within ten minutes. The excitement of the evening began to wear off, and she felt her eyes begin to droop as she approached the driveway between the house and the library. Her headlights flared across the library windows, but it wasn't until she shut off the engine and opened her door that she realized she'd heard a sound—breaking glass.

Her weariness vanished in a flash, and she saw a dark figure leap over the wall of her patio. Before she could register what she'd seen, the person was gone.

She grabbed the heavy flashlight she kept under her car seat and aimed it at the gate to the courtyard between the two buildings. It was standing open. She raced into the patio and aimed the light all around.

A window beside the back door to the library was

smashed. Was the intruder just arriving when she got home? Or had he already been inside? And, was he alone?

Chapter 34

Sam put the last swipe of chocolate icing on a tray of brownies for the display case out front and handed them off to Jen just as her phone rang. Emily.

"Hey, did you get a lot of reading done last night?" she asked.

"Well … yes and no. Someone broke into the library."

"What!"

"Yeah, I'd been over to Kelly's—another big story—and when I got home, I caught them in the act."

"Are you okay? Is the library okay?"

"Remember the uneasy feeling I've had about someone watching me? Now I have to wonder if this was their plan all along. I'm settling down, finally. I called the sheriff's department right away and Rico was here in about thirty seconds." Emily gave a shaky laugh. "A back window was broken and they'd reached in to unlock the back door. I still need to go through and see if anything's missing. At least, thank God, they didn't vandalize the place. There are horror stories of libraries with water and fire damage."

"Oh, sweetie, I can't imagine. Do you want me to come over and help you check things?"

"Sure, if you'd like. Kelly's on the way. She had to get Scott off to Albuquerque, and she's parking Ana with a friend for the day. So, yeah, anytime you can break away. But don't feel like you *must* come. Entirely optional."

"You said something about another big story?"

"Oh, that. We learned that Gabriel had a little love triangle going. If you want more detail, then yes, get over here."

Sam laughed and promised to be there as soon as she placed her supply order. Becky could handle the decorating orders, and Julio already had the morning pastries done and was in his element, mixing up dough for their seasonal cookies. Twenty minutes later, Sam was in her truck and on the way to the Morton Library.

She arrived just as Kelly was getting out of her car in the small parking lot.

"It's one thing after the other," Kelly said. "Makes me think we're getting close to figuring out this mystery. I just wish I knew which of the clues led in the right direction."

They found Emily in the back room, sweeping glass shards from the floor near the back door.

"Careful where you step," she warned. "I think I've got most of it, but you know how it is with broken glass."

"I can finish this," Sam said, setting her pack on a table, "if you want to start checking for missing items."

"I've already looked in my petty cash box. It's untouched. The only other thing of value in here is information. So, no enticement to the average person."

"That makes me think it was somehow connected to our investigation. There is almost *certainly* something in this building that will tell us who the killer was." Sam tried to think of who might want to get to the information before it could be used against them.

"We've talked to Maldonados, to a Ramos, to numerous people at the town archives and building departments. Even the real estate agent knew we were going out to the Graystone place. But I can't imagine who would think of the library as a target." Kelly walked over to the coffee maker, which was sputtering its grand finale. The carafe was full.

"I do leave a small nighttime lamp on in the front. Maybe they thought they'd catch me here," Emily said. "It was a bit after ten p.m. so if I had been here, it would have been a sure bet I was alone."

"You're thinking of the person who'd been following you," Kelly said, her face etched with concern.

"*Allegedly* following," Emily admitted. "Rico asked about that, and I had to say that it was more a feeling than actually spotting someone."

"Too bad you hadn't gotten a good look and could identify them," Sam said.

Emily dumped a dustpan full of glass in the wastebasket and looked around the room. "I don't know how I'm supposed to determine if anything was stolen. There's so much material here that has never been catalogued. But I told Rico I'd let him know if I figure it out. He wants to complete his report."

She gave a sigh and reached for the mug of coffee Kelly held out to her.

"Let's split up and see what we can find," Emily suggested. "Sam, why don't you start with the crate we brought back from Graystone, since you were there and saw what went into it. I'll check my records of materials that have been requested recently, although I seriously doubt a patron would come in the dead of night for something they could get simply by asking. Kel, maybe take a look through the section of old newspapers my grandfather had gathered, over there by the west wall."

Kelly sipped her coffee and looked around at the vast collection. This wasn't going to be easy.

Chapter 35

They worked for three hours, barely conversing as each woman immersed herself in the unmistakable scent of old books and forgotten secrets. Emily kept pondering what they'd read last night in Gabriel's diary. What other stories, she wondered, were hidden within this town? Whose lives had been forever changed by love, betrayal, and murder?

"Hey, Em!" Kelly called from across the room, beckoning her over. "Look at this!"

Emily carefully descended the ladder and joined her friend, who hovered over an old newspaper article. The headline read: **Maldonado Brothers Arrested for Illegal Gambling Operation**.

"Not their first brush with the law. Remember the other article about their connection to a string of robberies.

Could this be connected to our case?" Emily asked, her pulse quickening.

"Maybe we need to be looking at the bigger picture, at what else was going on around town. It could be that Gabriel was what they would call collateral damage in some other battle that was happening," Samantha mused, joining them.

"True," Kelly said. "Could be nothing at all to do with Clara."

"This article is dated just a few weeks before Gabriel's murder," Emily said. "It says here that Augustine and Antonio Maldonado were released on bail pending their trial. But there's no mention of the trial itself, or what happened afterward."

"Interesting," Kelly said, biting her lip. "So they had run-ins with the law before Gabriel's murder. That could definitely be relevant."

"Wait, look at this," Emily said, pointing to a small photograph in the corner of the newspaper page. It depicted a man with slicked-back dark hair and sharp features– Augustine Maldonado. "Doesn't he look familiar?" Emily asked, her heart pounding as she tried to place his face.

"Actually, now that you mention it…" Samantha trailed off, her eyes widening. "He looks just like that guy we saw at the farmer's market, the one who was haggling with the spice seller over her prices."

"Are you suggesting that Augustine Maldonado is still alive?" Kelly whispered, incredulous. "But that would make him over a hundred years old!"

"Has to be someone else," Emily decided, her mind racing. "A descendant, perhaps? Someone who might have inherited both Augustine's looks and his ill manners?"

"I'll ask around," Samantha said, "That spice merchant

is a friend. Maybe she can tell me more about this man. He could be key in some way." She fired off a quick text to the woman, asking her to call if she knew the man.

"Okay," Kelly said, her eyes shining. "Let's keep searching. We're so close, I can feel it!"

She'd no sooner spoken than her phone pinged with a text. She dug into her pocket and retrieved it. "Uh-oh. Ana got sick at her friend's house and wants to come home. I gotta go."

"Is she okay?" Sam asked.

Kelly was texting a quick reply. "I'm sure she will be. Having her daddy home for two days, well let's just say there were lots of extra treats, and I suspect they ate nearly a whole carton of ice cream together last night when I wasn't looking. I'm not surprised she's got a tummy ache."

Emily walked her to the door and locked it behind her. Stretching, she turned to Sam. "What about you? Doing okay? I can't believe how the whole morning got away. I can grab us some lunch if you're hungry."

"I could eat," Sam said, not taking her eyes off a folder she'd just pulled from a shelf labeled 'Taos Connections.'

"I'll run over to the house and rustle up something. I don't want to be gone when the glazier gets here to replace the broken window. For sure, I need that repaired before the day's over."

Sam's phone rang almost the minute Emily walked out the door. It was Sam's friend, the spice merchant.

"Hey, Sam, I got your message. Need something new this week?"

Sam explained her question about the man who'd been so obnoxious.

"Oh, no, sorry. I mean, I've seen him around. He's

somebody local but I don't know his name or anything else about him really."

"Okay, it was just a random lead I'm trying to track down."

"I'd be happy to let you know if I see him again or get any other information."

"That would be great," Sam told her friend. "And if you get any of those special dried cloves this week, I'll take a packet. I always go through lots in my Christmas baking."

They ended the call and Sam went back to her research.

Emily was back in a few minutes, with a plate of sandwiches, a bag of chips, two glasses of ice, and two sodas. "Take a break, Sam. You've been on your feet a lot of hours."

"Oh, I'm used to that," Sam assured her. She ducked into the library's tiny bathroom and washed the dust from her hands. When she returned, she reported on the phone call then sank onto one of the chairs at the table and sighed. "But I have to say, this feels good and the sandwiches look yummy."

"Ham and cheese was what I had. Take your pick of the Coke or the Sprite. I figured something bubbly would help wake me up. Getting a little bleary eyed at this point in the day."

"You had a late night." Sam popped the top on the Coke and poured it over ice.

"Late and scary. I find myself glancing up at the windows to see if anyone's around. I gotta get past this, thinking there are shadows everywhere."

"Maybe. Just be careful. There really are bad guys in this world."

"Definitely. But I feel so much safer in a small town

than I did in the big city." Emily picked up half a sandwich and bit in. With a cheek full, she continued. "Maybe I'm blending past and present, in my mind, thinking the bad guys from the past could still be lurking around. And I know that's silly."

Sam's gaze fell to the folder she'd been going through, the Taos connections. "Just before you came back with lunch, I was going through this," she said, pulling it over, "and I came across your name."

"What?"

"Plankhurst, I mean. William P. Plankhurst."

"My great-grandfather. He would have been alive during the time we're looking at, the early 1900s. What did it say about him?"

"Not sure. I was just getting to that part. A lot of the pages in the folder, I noticed, seem to be sort of a who's who. Some sheets are family trees. It's a variety." She set her sandwich down and picked up the folder. "I can probably find it ..."

Emily sipped at her Sprite and watched in interest.

"Okay, yeah, here it is." She pulled out a sheet of old, deckled paper on which was drawn a traditional tree-shaped genealogy and handed it to Emily.

"Ah yes, I may have seen this before. Grandma Valerie had a copy of it. Hm, it might have been in this old trunk she kept in the spare bedroom in the house."

She ran her finger down the names on the left-hand branches, then those on the right. "Oh. My. Gosh."

Sam looked up. "What's wrong?"

Emily raised her eyes and stared. "I think I'm related to Iris Maxwell."

It was Sam's turn to look astonished.

"Very distantly. So distant, I'm not sure what you'd call it. But look here. There's my great-grandfather's name." She pointed at a branch on the left side. "And over here are the Maxwells—Iris is one of the grandchildren on that side. They would have been distant cousins, third or fourth or something …"

"Do you think your grandfather, um, great-grandfather actually knew her?"

"I have no idea." Emily's face had gone pale. "It's beyond coincidence, don't you think? What if Gabriel specifically sought me out because he knows of this connection?"

Chapter 36

Emily sat in her grandfather's study, tapping a finger on the desk, her thoughts roiling with everything she'd learned. She'd washed her face and brushed her teeth, donned a t-shirt for sleep, and planned to get to bed early tonight, but her mind just wouldn't settle.

"This is ridiculous!" she muttered.

She stood and slipped a pair of sweats and a cardigan over the t-shirt. Maybe some warm milk—wasn't that what her grandmother used to give her? She padded to the kitchen and looked in the fridge, poured milk into a mug, and set it in the microwave. While it circled for a minute, she looked around the room.

"Grandma Valerie, are you there?"

Nothing.

"Please? I just have some questions."

The faint shape of her grandmother materialized, rubbing her eyes as her image became clearer.

"You look sleepy," Emily said as the microwave beeped.

"Well, yes, dear. We ghosts need our rest, too."

Emily tested the milk with a tentative sip. "I learned something today and it's been disturbing my sleep."

"The warm milk is just the right thing, dear."

"We'll see. Actually, can I ask you … Did our family know the Graystones personally? I found a family tree that indicates we're related distantly to the Maxwells. And other evidence shows the Maxwells knew the Graystones. This would have been in the time of Morton Plankhurst, and probably William. Do you know anything about that?"

Valerie held up both hands and stepped back. "Sorry, before my time. William was my husband's father and he'd passed away before we married. I never knew him. And Morton … your great-great-grandfather … well, that was very much ancient history before I came into this family."

Emily felt her mood drop. "Okay, I just thought it might be worth a chance to see if you knew anything about the connections."

"Finish your milk, sweetheart, and get some rest. Maybe things will be clearer in the morning." With that, Valerie faded away.

Emily sipped the warm drink, closing her eyes in hopes of feeling sleepy, but it didn't work. She set the empty mug in the kitchen sink and walked through the house. Through the living room window she stared toward the library, its secrets tugging at her. She pulled on her sneakers and grabbed her keys, then headed in that direction.

She knew where she was going, even before her mind made the conscious decision.

It took less than a minute to let herself into the library,

another few seconds to reach the bookcase with the trigger that opened the doorway to the tunnel. And although she knew it was no certain thing that she would find Gabriel there, as she picked up a flashlight she found herself hoping she would encounter his handsome face once again.

Don't be dumb about this, she cautioned herself. *It's foolish to find yourself attracted to a ghost. Stay tough.*

Emily stood in the dimly lit tunnel, feeling the dusty earth beneath her shoes and hearing the soft echoes of the past.

"Gabriel? Are you here?"

Her eyes scanned the dimly lit passage ahead of her. "Gabriel?"

He appeared all at once, unlike Valerie who tended to arrive slowly.

"I'm glad you came back," he said, giving her a tender look.

Emily clenched her fists at her sides as she stared at his translucent form, casting an eerie glow in the darkness.

"Tell me about Iris Maxwell," she demanded, her voice tight. "You were having an affair with her, weren't you? Was my great-grandfather somehow in the picture?"

Gabriel shifted uncomfortably, his ghostly eyes darting away from Emily's piercing gaze. "Iris was … a mistake. I never meant for it to happen." He sighed, the sound like a mournful whisper echoing around them. "Your great-grandfather was her cousin, but he didn't know about our affair."

Emily's heart raced as he confirmed what she had suspected, her mind a whirlwind of thoughts and questions. "Are you certain about that?" she asked, desperation tinging her voice. "As one of her male cousins, maybe he felt honor bound to teach you a lesson. Could he have been involved in your murder?"

"Perhaps," Gabriel admitted hesitantly. "I don't know for certain. But I do know that I feared the consequences of what I had done—from one of the families or the other."

He hung his head. "After I realized that my body was dead, I wanted justice for myself, even if I didn't deserve it."

"Justice?" Emily scoffed, anger boiling within her. "You were cheating on Clara with her friend! You were planning to marry her while seeing Iris behind her back!"

"I know!" Gabriel snapped, his face contorted with anguish. "I know how terrible it all was, and I've spent decades regretting my actions. But I also know that I didn't deserve to die for my mistakes."

"Maybe not," Emily conceded, her anger subsiding slightly. "But you can't expect me to just accept this without trying to find the truth. My family's history, my great-grandfather's legacy, the entire Morton Library … Now I learn it's all tied up in this mystery, and I need to know how deep it goes."

"Of course," Gabriel replied, his voice softer now. "I understand your need for answers, Emily. And I will do what I can to help you find them."

"Gabriel, what's the *real* reason you broke it off with Clara?" Emily asked, her blue eyes searching his face for any sign of deception.

"Emily, I loved Clara deeply, but marrying her would have only fueled the feud between our families," Gabriel explained, sorrow etched on his ghostly features. "I wanted to end the fighting and bring peace to those I cared about."

"In what way? I'm so confused! I hear that there was this dumb feud, but then some say the two families saw your marriage as a good liaison."

"There's more … other facts you don't know yet."

"So, tell me."

"Both families wanted political power, and in this state politics and money go together."

"I was under the impression both families were well off."

His eyes darted down the tunnel, as if he were listening for anyone who might overhear. "Yes, somewhat. There had been land deals, mining interests, but the Maldonados had run through much of their fortune. My family still had the Graystone treasure."

Emily felt as if the ground had dropped away. "Treasure? What treasure—why am I just now hearing about this?"

"My father and uncles found a great deal of gold in one of the mines. They took it, hid it, and vowed not to reveal its existence until the time was exactly right."

"And when would that be …?"

"My father's plan for me was that I would become governor of the state, and eventually would be elected president of the United States. That would require funding. Meanwhile, the Maldonados would run out of money before they could produce a serious rival."

"But your marriage to Clara Maldonado would bring the two families together and everyone would benefit from the political prestige?"

"It seemed so to anyone else, but no one consulted me. I loved Clara, but I hated the politics. On the few occasions I attended official functions in Santa Fe with my father, I felt an abhorrence for the entire process. I could not imagine myself in that lifestyle. I wanted to live on the land, raise animals, pursue my artwork. People said I had a real talent for it. No Santa Fe politics for me, and certainly no life in Washington, DC, in the future."

"Okay, I get that. But breaking off with Clara, breaking her heart and yours? Did you really think having an affair with Iris would accomplish what you wanted?" she retorted, crossing her arms over her chest.

"Of course not," he sighed. "I made a terrible mistake, and it cost me my life. I only … only … Oh, Emily, I just need answers." He collapsed to his knees, sobbing, as his image faded away.

Chapter 37

Emily stumbled out of the tunnel, drained by the emotion of the encounter. By the time she closed the bookcase and locked the library, she was more than ready to fall into bed. When she woke it was midmorning, sunlight hitting her pillow.

"Ugh, no, I don't want to get up," she moaned. Then she remembered the treasure.

She dragged herself to the shower and dressed before calling Kelly. "You will not believe what I learned last night. There's a Graystone treasure. Can you come? And be ready for a trip into the tunnels."

"Ohmygosh, Mom would love that. But she's pretty busy this morning, so I'll leave Ana with her at the bakery, and I'll bring the wooden box," her friend promised. "Thirty, forty minutes?"

"Perfect." Emily ended the call and fortified herself with a breakfast of sliced ham and a scrambled egg.

Kelly drove up just as she was finishing. She wore jeans and a UNM sweatshirt that looked like it had seen better days.

"A treasure? What the—?"

"I know. Crazy, right?" Emily recapped the confrontation with Gabriel over his decision to break up with Clara, and his revelation that politics and money were behind the whole mess. "The main thing I didn't think to ask him was the obvious question—where are these riches?"

"So you think it's still around? Seems like someone would have taken it, that it would be long gone by now."

"We need to find out. The answers may be down there, or they may be in the past. Are you ready for that?"

"*So* ready! I think that's the key to solving this mystery."

"Agreed," Emily said, her thoughts turning to the task at hand. "I have the feeling the bounty is hidden somewhere in the tunnels under Taos, but we don't know exactly where or how to access it. If we can connect with Gabriel again, he may be able to tell us something."

"Good idea," Kelly agreed, holding up the carved box. "And this—just in case."

"Right," Emily said, taking a deep breath. "Let's get to work."

"Gabriel," she asked quietly as they studied the sketch of the tunnel system, "we could use a little help here."

His transparent shape appeared.

Kelly gripped Emily's arm. "Yes, he's quite real," Emily assured her. "You can breathe now."

Kelly drew a deep breath and smiled at the ghost, who gave a gentlemanly little nod.

Emily turned to Gabriel once more. "First, I need you to show us the way to wherever the Graystone treasure is hidden. I'm assuming that will require us to go through the time portal?"

"It would be best," he acknowledged. "The last I knew on this subject, it was hidden beneath a secret floor panel in the mansion that's accessible from the tunnel."

"But—how is that huge old house connected to the tunnel system? It's pretty far away."

"There is one tunnel, a very long and narrow one, that connects the mansion with the tunnels in town."

Kelly spoke up. "Are we sure such a long tunnel would still be intact after all these years?"

"I don't know," Gabriel admitted. "But it's worth trying. If you are traveling in the year 1920, it should be open."

Both women nodded. Kelly tucked the wooden box into her small daypack.

"I can't say for certain," he admitted, his eyes dark with concern. "But I know that you and Kelly are strong and resourceful. And together, you shall figure this out."

"Uh, thanks," Emily replied. "Okay, lead the way."

Emily and Kelly followed him into the dark tunnel, their flashlights casting eerie shadows on the walls as they followed his direction. Emily's heart raced as she thought of what they might discover this time. Kelly stuck right with them.

Gabriel led them through a series of twists and turns, and he was correct—after the fierce breeze that indicated they'd crossed into the past, the condition of the tunnels improved. In the distance, they could hear music from the speakeasy, but he directed them away from it, pointing out their progress on the map Emily carried with her. Once they'd passed the steps that would lead up to the kitchen of the Hotel La Fonda, he directed them to keep going easterly.

"Here is where I leave you," he said. "Turn this corner and then stay with the smaller tunnel. It will seem like a long way. You are traveling more than a mile in distance."

Emily looked a little shaky, but Kelly pulled the box from her pack and let it warm her hands. "We can do this," she said, replacing it.

"Of that, I have no doubt," Gabriel said, offering her a ghostly smile before vanishing once again into the shadows.

"I'm sticking close," Kelly whispered, "and trying to be ready for anything."

As they turned the corner, they both heard a sound behind them. The beams of their flashlights revealed three figures. Augustine and Antonio Maldonado and Nathaniel Graystone were blocking their exit, their faces twisted into menacing snarls.

Chapter 38

"Oh crap," Kelly said. Emily's face had gone whiter than ever.

"Look who's here," Augustine sneered, his slicked-back hair gleaming in the dim light. "The little detectives. You—" He pointed at Emily. "I spotted you eavesdropping in the bar, snooping around. What are you playing at?"

"What do you want?" Emily demanded, trying to keep her voice steady despite the pounding of her heart.

"Simple," Antonio replied, his eyes cold and calculating. "We want justice for our sister. Where is Gabriel?"

Now Emily knew why Gabriel had sent them on alone. In this timeframe he hadn't died yet. His ghost couldn't be here. She studied the angry faces on the men. This was about more than a broken engagement. These three wanted the treasure.

"Your idea of *justice* is twisted," Kelly shot back, her green eyes flashing with anger. "You're just as responsible for the feud as anyone else!"

"Enough!" Nathaniel barked, stepping forward and raising a threatening fist. "You will not stand in our way!"

"Stop right there!" Sam's voice rang out from behind them, her carved wooden box clutched tightly in one hand. Her gray hair was disheveled, but her eyes blazed as she rushed to Emily and Kelly's side. "I won't let you harm them!"

"Mom?" Kelly said with wide eyes. "Where's Ana?"

"Safe with Becky at the bakery," Sam whispered. "I had a feeling about this, that you'd need extra help. I made it through the library portal just before it closed."

Augustine apparently picked up on the library connection, cocking his head and squinting at Emily. "You look very much like William Plankhurst, the man with the collection of books. A relative of his?" He exchanged a look with his brother and a wicked grin spread across his face.

"Just the woman we were hoping to see."

"Leave my family alone!" Sam shouted, stepping protectively in front of the girls.

"Or what?" Antonio challenged, smirking at Sam's show of courage.

"Or you'll have to answer to all of us!" Sam declared. She held her wooden box tightly, ready to use its powers against the three men blocking their way.

"Back off," Emily warned, her mouth in a snarl.

"Three *women*. This is no match," Augustine sneered, lunging toward Sam.

She sidestepped his grip, her wooden box glowing brighter in response to the danger. She muttered an incantation under her breath, and a whirlwind of energy burst forth from the box, narrowly missing the other Maldonado brother as he charged toward her, a knife in one hand.

Sam spun, not letting him out of her sight.

"Kelly, watch out!" Emily yelled, tackling her friend to the ground just as Nathaniel swung a heavy iron pipe at them. The chilling sound of metal connecting with a heavy wooden beam echoed through the tunnel. Emily shuddered to think what would have happened had she not intervened in time.

"Emily, grab my hand!" Kelly called out between ragged breaths, her fingers lightly touching Sam's, drawing energy from her mother. As Emily grasped her friend's hand, a warm current flowed through her veins, and she felt a surge of renewed strength. They spun to face their attackers head-on.

Antonio held the knife, poised on the balls of his feet and ready to spring. Sam unleashed another burst of energy from the box, and his arm flew backward. The hand holding the knife smacked a wooden beam and the knife bounced to the ground. Emily grabbed it.

But Nathaniel still had the iron pipe and his reach was longer than hers. He advanced on the three women, his face a mask of anger.

No sign of the future state senator there, Kelly thought in a moment that felt a little out-of-body.

Augustine was scanning the area, looking for a weapon. Both of the Maldonados were keeping behind Nathaniel Graystone and the iron pipe.

"Enough of this!" Sam shouted. Combating the men with bursts of energy from the box would likely only work one more time. "Girls, we're getting out of here, now!"

"Right behind you!" Emily agreed, her heart pounding as adrenaline coursed through her.

Sam aimed all of her energy toward the arm holding the iron pipe and sent it whirling through the air, narrowly missing Antonio's head. As all three men dodged the projectile, she screamed for Emily and Kelly to get past them.

Emily led the way, Kelly right on her heels.

Sam turned to follow when Nathaniel snarled, launching at Sam with a vicious kick that sent her sprawling to the ground. The box tumbled from her grasp, its glow waning as it skittered across the cold, damp earth.

"Sam!" Emily cried, fighting back tears as she saw her friend lying motionless on the ground. She grabbed up the fallen wooden box.

A piercing shriek split the air, the high-pitched scream of a child.

"Ana!" Kelly screamed. "How did you get here?" She raced to her child, grabbing her up in her arms.

"Get to the exit!" Sam croaked, her voice barely audible as she struggled to rise. "I'll hold them off!"

"We're not leaving without you!" Kelly shouted. She reached for Sam's hand, sending her own renewed energy into her mother. She drew Sam to her feet. "Come on. We can do this."

Emily picked up the box Sam had dropped, then pulled a very weakened Sam along, while Kelly hugged Ana to her chest. They passed through the strong wind of the time portal and the sounds of their pursuers vanished.

"I think my ankle's broken. Leave me here," Sam gasped, her face white with pain. "You three get out, bring back help." She sank down into a tiny alcove in the wall.

"Keep this!" Kelly said, swallowing back tears as she placed the carved box on Sam's lap. "Mom? I don't want to leave you like this."

"Go—just get yourselves and Ana out safely." Sam held the box tightly. "I'll be okay."

"We must be near the doorway to the La Fonda's kitchen," Emily told them. "That's where we'll send help, the hotel."

Chapter 39

Kelly and Emily emerged from the dark, suffocating confines of the tunnel, collapsing on the grass outside as exhaustion and fear threatened to overwhelm them. They were battered and bruised, but alive. For now. She touched Ana's little face, running her hands over her child's arms and legs.

"How did you get down there, baby? Why weren't you at the bakery?"

"I'm not a baby! And I just followed Grammie. I know the way to Auntie Emily's library." Ana exuded bravado, but didn't let go of Kelly.

"Wait—we're not in the hotel kitchen. Where did we come out?" Emily muttered, staring around.

They were in the center of the Plaza, the bandstand to their left and the public restrooms nearby. The wrought iron railing that surrounded the town square was in place, as were the tall cottonwoods and other plantings. At least they were in their own time once again.

"My mom ... Is she in the past still or in our time?" Kelly whispered, with worry etched into every line of her face.

Emily reached out and squeezed her hand. "Our time, I'm pretty sure. *I really hope.*"

"We'll find a way to save her," Kelly vowed, her voice hoarse. "We can't let them get away with this."

"Agreed," Emily said, rubbing a spot where Nathaniel Graystone's iron weapon had grazed her arm. She stuffed the map of the tunnels into her pocket. "But let's take care of Ana and get Sam out of there first."

Kelly pulled out her cell phone, waiting for a signal. She reached Jen, who was in tears.

"I'm so sorry, Kel, we've been searching everywhere. I was frantic."

"Ana's fine. She wandered after Mom when she left the bakery. And she knows she is *never* to do that again," Kelly said, sending a significant look toward her daughter.

Knowing they still had a lot ahead of them, she asked Jen if she could come to the Plaza and get Ana. Jen said she was already on her way out the door. She could cover the short block in a couple of minutes.

"And this time you will not leave the bakery until either Grammie or I come to get you," she said to Ana.

At last, Kelly was able to call Sheriff Evan and give their location. "My mom may have a broken ankle, down in one of those underground tunnels."

"Geez, Kelly, what the hell?" But he promised to send help as quickly as he could.

"Em, I'm going through the hotel kitchen and find

Mom," Kelly said, once she'd handed off Ana to Jen with stern instructions to stay put. "I'll let her know we've got help on the way, and I'll stay with her until they come."

She found Sam exactly where they'd left her. The wooden box was glowing, and Sam was breathing a little raggedly. "I've never seen that reaction from the box before," she whispered to Kelly. "That rush—whatever that power was. It must have sensed the danger and come to defend us. Literally. The good news is that I'm not feeling any pain at all."

"I know. It was bizarre." Kelly held out a hand. "Come on, let's go."

They made their way up the steps to the hotel kitchen and into the lobby.

A sheriff's cruiser and an ambulance arrived three minutes later, and none of the women wanted to admit they'd used special powers to heal Sam's injuries. They let the professionals take over. Within a few minutes, they had Sam inside the ambulance.

"It's feeling better now," Sam assured everyone. "It might only be a sprain, but I'll go to the hospital to have it checked out."

She looked deeply into Kelly's eyes, whispering. "I want you two to go back down there and find that … you know, what we were looking for. The Maldonados are after it, and there's no way we can explain the whole time-travel experience to these guys," she said with a nod toward the deputy. "Go now, take the box with you. I'll be fine."

"All right, if you're sure," Emily agreed, her voice shaky but resolute.

"I'm sure. They'll find nothing wrong with my ankle and I'll be out of there in an hour or two. I'll give you a call."

Kelly and Emily watched the ambulance drive away. Kelly let out a shaky breath. "Whew, rough morning. Let's walk back to the library and decide what to do next."

Emily squeezed her hand. "Your mom is right about getting the Maldonado brothers. Those two really are monsters."

"Let's not forget about Nathaniel," Kelly interjected. "We had no idea he was working with Augustine and Antonio. How does he fit into all this?"

"Right," Emily said, her eyes narrowing in anger. "And, how does this connect to the Graystone treasure?"

"I'm guessing it all goes back to the feud between the families," Kelly suggested, as they crossed Camino de la Placita and headed toward Emily's place.

"Maybe," Emily admitted, mulling over the idea. "But we need more information. What else did Gabriel mention?"

"Didn't he say that he saw someone else at the scene of his murder?" Kelly wondered, her voice hesitating for a moment. "Someone who could have been the real killer?"

"He told me he doesn't remember. Bent Street was pretty deserted at night. But, now we know that the Graystone treasure is also somehow linked to everything that's happened. Nathaniel," Emily murmured, her mind racing. "He must be after it too, or maybe he's trying to protect a secret."

"I have this feeling we've got enough information to solve the mystery now," Kelly said, as they approached Emily's house and she saw both of their cars parked there. "We just need to put all the pieces together."

"Right," Emily agreed. "Let's figure this out and take down those Maldonado brothers once and for all."

Chapter 40

There's a little practical matter we'll have to address," Emily said, once they'd let themselves into the library. "The Maldonados who attacked us in the tunnel this morning actually exist in 1920. We can't exactly dash back there with our sheriff and have him arrest them."

Kelly grinned. "No kidding. Can you imagine no-nonsense Evan's reaction when we tell him he has to time-travel and pick up a couple of thugs, a hundred years ago?"

"So, I've been thinking how to handle that, and here's my idea. We go back down there, travel back to their time, and find the sheriff of the day. We convince 1920-sheriff of our story and have him pick them up."

"We'd be changing history …" Kelly said with a sideways look at her friend.

Emily tapped her foot for a moment, thinking.

"Wouldn't that happen only if the sheriff from the past found them guilty and they were executed for murdering Gabriel? If things play out as they should, he will question them about hiring Ramos to commit the murder. He will then question Tomas and learn that he didn't do it …"

"But while he has them detained in jail, we have the chance to follow Gabriel's instructions and locate the Graystone treasure."

"Exactly!" Emily gave her a triumphant fist-bump.

"Providing we don't run into Nathaniel in the process. He would most certainly fight to keep the gold himself."

"And maybe that's how history goes," Emily said. "Maybe that's the money the family used to buy their way to some top political positions over the years."

"What will be, will be. Right?"

"To the tunnels! Bring the wooden box with you, and your flashlight." Emily led the way toward the bookcase entrance. "Oh, let's come up with some clothes that will help us fit in."

She rummaged in a back closet where she'd stashed donations to the library. Once in a while someone brought boxes of historical things that weren't necessarily paper. She came up with a long skirt for Kelly and a slouch hat for herself. Tucking her hair up inside it, and wearing a baggy jacket over her other clothes, she might pass for a teen boy. Kelly donned the skirt over her jeans and found a knitted scarf that could serve as a shawl. She picked up a cloth bag that would look more natural than her modern daypack.

"Ready?"

"As I'll ever be," Kelly said with a smile.

The descent down the stone steps and into the earthen tunnel was beginning to feel familiar, and they made their way to the spot where the time portal activated. Almost immediately, they heard music and laughter from the speakeasy

"What better place to locate the town sheriff," Emily said. "I hear local law enforcement was pretty lax about the Prohibition laws out West."

"If he's not here, it's still a great place to ask questions."

They pushed through the door and found themselves in a short hallway that led into the noisy bar. Although it was mid-afternoon in their world, down here it seemed that the night was in full swing. More than a dozen patrons stood at the bar, men sporting evening wear and women in sequined, fringed dresses with plenty of leg showing and flashy makeup.

"I feel kind of dowdy in a long skirt," Kelly muttered.

"It's okay. Look young. We're just a couple of teens looking for help for our parents."

"Uh, right. Whatever."

Emily got right into the role and approached a table where two couples sat, people who were dressed a bit less conspicuously than those at the bar. "Excuse me, sir. Ma'am. Our parents didn't come home tonight and we need the sheriff's help. Is he in here somewhere?"

She got a sideways glance from one couple, but the other woman spoke up. "You kids okay?"

"Yes, ma'am, we'll be fine. Just need to talk with the sheriff."

"Um, well, all right. You see the man at the far end of the bar? The one with the white hat?"

Kelly almost laughed at the cliché description, but when she looked she did, indeed, see a man in a white hat.

"Well, that ain't him, but he's a deputy and he'll be able

to tell you where Sheriff Fineman is."

"Thank you very much, ma'am," Emily said, taking Kelly's elbow like a protective brother would do.

By the time they made their way through the crowded room, the deputy had been joined by another man, this one wearing black pants and a leather vest, on which a badge was clearly visible. The sheriff seemed to be convincing his deputy that it was time to leave.

The girls hung back, letting the men converse, then followed when they walked through an exit door on the opposite end of the room from where the tunnel had brought them. They were standing on a wooden sidewalk, in front of the adobe walls of the shops that lined the Plaza. Gaslights circled the perimeter, giving the square a cozy glow in the darkness. Horses were tied to a hitching post. Several carriages sat in an open lot at the end of the block, and two motorcars were parked at the verge.

Once the heavy speakeasy door had closed behind them, Emily called out, "Sheriff Fineman?"

The man turned. "Yes, son. What can I do for you?"

Emily put a little hitch in her voice. "We were attacked, earlier today. Us and our mama. It was the Maldonado brothers, sir."

Kelly instantly understood. Keep the story somewhat close to the truth. "Yes, sir, that's right. They got downright ugly about it. One of 'em swung an iron pipe at Mama."

"Where did this happen?" the sheriff demanded, standing taller and placing a hand on the grip of his sidearm.

"Down in the tunnels, sir," Emily said. "We was going from our shop over on the Camino, making our way toward a place where Mama stores some of her merchandise, and they just jumped out at us."

Kelly began to fear that the details would be their undoing, that the sheriff would want to know which shop was their mother's and where, exactly, this attack had taken place. But the two men were looking at each other.

"Damn Maldonados," Fineman muttered. "At it again."

"Okay, kids, don't you worry," the deputy said. "We don't take kindly to anyone intimidatin' our citizens. We'll find them. You go on home now."

The young women turned away and heard Fineman's voice behind them. "Thugs. They may be rich, but they're thugs anyway."

Emily squeezed Kelly's hand, and the two of them strolled casually toward the hotel.

Chapter 41

They walked into the lobby of the La Fonda, pausing a moment to take in the changes, how the modern Southwestern motif now held Victorian era furniture, and the reception desk had been moved.

"The kitchen has to be in the back, even a hundred years ago," Emily whispered.

"And surely the basement and tunnel entrance haven't changed." Kelly had been through here a few hours ago, rescuing Sam, but everything looked different from the perspective of history. She pointed toward the dining room. "Through there, I think."

The prime dinner hour seemed to be over. A few customers lingered over coffee, and waiters were clearing tables. The two walked through the room without receiving much attention, spotting a set of double swinging doors at the far end, partially concealed by a screen. Kelly tilted her head toward it and they adjusted course.

A man wearing a stained white jacket and tall chef's hat gave them a hard look, but someone called out to him and when he turned his head, they skittered toward the doorway at the other end of the crowded kitchen.

They ducked through and bounded down the stairs to the basement.

"There," Emily whispered, pointing to a door in the wall on their left. "I'm pretty sure that's it."

The heavy wooden door offered some resistance but they pushed it open and stepped through, closing it behind them.

"Flashlights!" Kelly squealed, not liking the total darkness. "Okay, better."

They shined the beams around, getting their bearings.

"One thing about old tunnels, they don't change a whole lot," Kelly said. "This short section will lead us to where we were earlier today, then we can follow Gabriel's instructions to make the long trek out to his family home."

"Why didn't we just request the key from the Realtor again and make the drive out there? Go at it from the top?" Emily asked after they'd oriented themselves and were on the right path.

"One, we had to send the sheriff after the Maldonados. And two, we don't know where inside Graystone Manor this tunnel comes out. We found a basement room, but aside from old furnishings and papers, I didn't spot any valuables."

"No gold, for sure," Emily agreed. "If the gold is still there, it wasn't just sitting in a room someplace."

They both got quiet. It could be, after all these years, that there was no gold. Maybe there never had been. The whole story could just be a legend.

The smell of damp earth filled their nostrils. Kelly's hair began to frizz and stick to her forehead. She wondered if they'd passed near a creek or waterway.

"Can you feel it?" Kelly whispered, her voice echoing down the long, narrow passageway. "The history … it's like the walls have secrets."

Emily brushed away a cobweb that had strayed across her face. She focused on the uneven ground beneath her feet as she tried to ignore the way the shadows seemed to dance around them, hinting at unseen dangers lurking just out of sight. Every so often, she would catch herself glancing over her shoulder. Since the encounter with the Maldonados, the feeling of being watched had returned.

"Gabriel talked about a hidden chamber," Kelly said, scanning the walls for any sign of an entrance. "If we can find it, maybe we'll find the Graystone treasure."

"Or Nathaniel and the Maldonado brothers, if the sheriff didn't catch up with them," Emily added, her voice tense. "We need to be careful."

"Right," Kelly agreed, gripping her flashlight tighter.

The sound of their footsteps echoed down the tunnel, but as they continued deeper, Emily could have sworn she heard other footsteps mingling with their own. Was it just her imagination? Or were they not alone?

"Kelly," Emily whispered, stopping in her tracks. The other sounds didn't stop. "Do you hear that?"

Kelly paused, listening intently. Her eyes widened. "Footsteps."

"Someone's following us," Emily said, her heart rate quickening. They exchanged uneasy looks, suddenly aware of the danger they were in. But who could it be? Augustine?

Antonio? Nathaniel? Or perhaps someone else entirely?

"Let's keep moving," Kelly urged, her voice hushed. "We'll deal with whoever it is when the time comes."

"All right," Emily agreed, her eyes scanning their surroundings for anything they could use to defend themselves.

The tunnel continued to twist and turn, leading them deeper into the unknown. The smell of damp earth grew stronger, filling their lungs with each breath. The air was thick with tension as they moved cautiously forward, hyper-aware of every sound and shadow.

"Emily, look!" Kelly exclaimed, pointing at a small opening in the wall. "Could that be the place?"

"Only one way to find out," Emily replied, her heart pounding against her ribcage. "Let's go in," she said, bracing herself.

"Wait," Kelly whispered, her voice strained. "I think … I think someone's already in there."

"Who?" Emily asked, trying to peer past her friend.

"I don't know," Kelly admitted, her grip on the flashlight tightening. "But I can hear breathing."

"Stay close," Emily warned, her body tensed and ready for action.

Together, they stood in the doorway to the hidden chamber and shone their lights around the open space, their hearts pounding in their chests. A shadow moved; Emily swore it was the same person who'd been watching them. Taking a step forward, a shiver went down her spine.

"Who are you?" Emily demanded, her voice shaking with a mixture of anger and fear.

"Show yourself!" Kelly added, her flashlight beam faltering in the darkness a moment before both of their lights died.

Behind them a heavy door slammed shut, echoing through the chamber, plunging them into darkness, and trapping them with the unknown person who had been watching their every move.

Chapter 42

Emily pounded her flashlight against her open palm, jostling the batteries and bringing its weak bulb back to life. She looked up and gasped. Across the room from them stood a young woman, her black, piercing eyes fixed on them, yet she remained silent. She wore a deep burgundy dress of fine material, knee-length, and a long strand of pearls draped twice around her neck. Her bobbed hair and marcel waves told them instantly that they were still in the 1920s.

"Iris Maxwell?" Kelly's voice came out steady despite the pounding of her heart.

The apparition tilted her head.

"We know about you and Gabriel Graystone. We're here to find the answers about his death, for his sake."

Iris's lips curled into a sneer. "And what makes you

think you have any idea about Gabriel's death?"

"We've been researching it," answered Emily, her eyes never wavering from the other woman's. "We've found quite a lot of evidence."

Kelly stepped forward. "The secret is out, Iris. We found Gabriel's diary and your letter to him, professing your love. He admits to your affair, but also says that he truly loved Clara. We also found letters detailing the Maldonado brothers' failed attempt to have Gabriel killed because he refused to marry their sister."

"Impossible!" Iris hissed, her face a mask of shock and anger. "Those letters were hidden away!"

"Nothing stays hidden forever," Emily replied. "Between the documents we've found and studied, and the use of certain, um, artifacts, we've uncovered a lot of the history. We know the Maldonados hired Tomas Ramos, but he didn't follow through with the murd—"

"*Magical* artifacts?" Iris interrupted, but her eyes betrayed a flicker of fear.

"Yes," said Kelly, meeting her eyes steadily.

"Gabriel's spirit reached out to us for help," Emily continued. "He wants to be released from his torment, and we're going to make sure that happens."

"Even if we have to go through you," added Kelly, feeling a fierce loyalty to her mother and friend, praying that her voice didn't shake.

Iris swallowed hard, clearly unnerved. She stared at the wooden box Kelly had pulled from her bag, as if she recognized its power.

"Work with us, Iris," Emily pleaded. "Help us discover what really happened. For Gabriel. You loved him. He needs to know what happened. Don't you want to see him at peace, finally?"

Iris paced to the opposite end of the hidden room. When she turned back to them, her lip trembled and tears glistened in her eyes. "It's only for Gabriel that I tell you this."

She paused. Emily and Kelly exchanged a glance. Was the woman really going to reveal anything at all? Emily approached, reaching out to touch her arm, when Iris broke down and fell to her knees on the earthen floor.

"It was an accident. I never meant to hurt him."

"An accident?" Emily's eyes were searching Iris's face for any hint of deception.

"Gabriel and I were lovers, that's true," Iris admitted, her voice barely a whisper as she tried to hold back tears. "I loved him deeply, but he chose Clara over me. In my despair, I walked out onto Bent Street late at night, the place known to harbor spirits of the past. I wanted to kill myself. I had brought a knife to slit my wrists, but he wrestled it away from me. Things got out of hand, and … I pushed him. He fell upon the knife and died."

A stunned silence filled the underground chamber. Finally, Emily turned to Kelly, staring. Behind her friend, another apparition appeared.

Gabriel.

His ghostly face was whiter than ever; clearly he was in shock.

Emily felt her heart go out to him. "Gabriel—wait! We need to hear more from Iris."

"I never remembered any of this," he moaned. Then he simply vanished.

Chapter 43

Young Iris wept into her hands as Emily and Kelly stood in stunned silence, eyes wide. What had just happened? Had they really solved the murder?

A sharp click sounded behind them and the heavy door to the chamber swung open. Iris looked up, leaped to her feet, and disappeared into the tunnels.

"What the ever-lovin' hell!" Kelly declared.

Emily's eyes were like saucers. "We need to get out—now!"

"I'm with you." Kelly turned back the way they had come, stumbling over the uneven ground in the wobbly light.

As they covered ground, their flashlight beams became stronger. They passed the tunnel entrance where they'd come through the hotel kitchen.

"I'd rather make it all the way to the library," Emily huffed. "Let's keep going."

When they rounded the final bend and recognized the stretch of tunnel where the library entry waited, a cold breeze wafted past them. Emily found herself watching for Gabriel's ghost, wondering if he was lingering, if he still had questions. But she saw no sign of him. Her heart ached in sympathy for his pain.

"Em? Uh, it's right here," Kelly said, pointing up the short flight of steps where she could see the opening in the bookcase.

They emerged into the library and looked around. Everything appeared as they had left it. They looked down at their makeshift period clothing.

"Gotta get out of these," Emily said, "but let's do it outside. There's enough dust among all my documents already."

Kelly gave a laugh that was a little too hearty, a mix of relief and nerves. "Did we just do what I think we did?"

"Iris Maxwell confessing to killing Gabriel, him overhearing her words? Yeah, it was way surreal."

They'd stepped out into the patio area, and Kelly was relieved to see their cars parked in their normal places. Back to the modern world.

They shook dust out of the vintage clothing and neatly folded everything.

"Now, what did I do with my cell phone?" Kelly asked, staring around, finally spotting her purse on the floor near the box of old clothes they'd raided earlier. "I should call Mom and find out how things went with her."

"What time is it, anyway?" Emily wondered. "I've completely lost track, but the sun's still up."

"Nearly three o'clock," Kelly answered.

She tapped Sam's number and breathed a sigh when Sam immediately picked up. "Beau came and picked me up at the hospital," she told her daughter. "We're on our way home now."

"Did you tell him what happened?" Kelly asked, cautiously.

"Everything pertinent," Sam said. "Look, we're picking up pizza. Shall we get enough for everyone?"

Kelly raised an eyebrow toward Emily, who nodded vigorously. "No way I'm cooking dinner tonight."

"That would be great," Kelly told Sam. "I'll pick up Ana and we'll come on over. There's some interesting news to share."

* * *

It was after pizza, when Beau took Ana out to the barn to help with some evening task, knowing full well that the women needed to talk, that Kelly and Emily spilled the whole story to Sam. Sending Sheriff Fineman after the Maldonado brothers, the scary trip through the tunnels, and hearing Iris's confession—it all came out in a tumble of words.

"I just don't know what to do next," Emily admitted. "It's tempting to go back to Graystone Manor and see if there truly is a treasure, as Gabriel described. But I can't let this whole thing go without talking to Iris again—present-day Iris."

"I agree," Kelly said, "And since we're dealing with a person who's over a hundred years old, I'm thinking we'd better get to her first thing tomorrow."

Sam gathered the paper plates they'd used for their

pizza. "If there was gold or something rare, somewhere in that house yesterday, it'll be there a few days from now."

The others agreed.

Emily's eyes grew misty. "I do hope the elderly version of Iris can offer something of comfort to Gabriel. I have a feeling he's going to show up again, and I don't know what to say to him."

Chapter 44

They drove up the mountainside to Iris's remote little home a little after midmorning, no one sure how to start the conversation. They were dealing with someone whose younger self admitted to a killing, but would the old woman accept that? She might deny it adamantly or claim to have no idea what they were talking about.

"Em, stop obsessing about what *might* happen," Sam counseled. "We won't know until we talk to her."

Emily stopped her Jeep outside the house and the three got out. Sam and Kelly had brought along their carved boxes, and they had the book of runes, all safely tucked inside Kelly's small daypack. They were, after all, dealing with a *bruja*—one who had admitted to a murder. Anything was possible.

Sophie admitted them to the house, gesturing toward

the living room where Iris sat in her chair with a hand-knitted afghan over her lap. For Emily and Kelly, it was a bit of a jolt recognizing the young woman from yesterday in this elderly, fragile condition.

"Hello, Iris, do you remember us?" Emily began.

"Well, of course I do," snapped the old woman in the chair. "It's my body that's giving out, not my mind."

"Can we talk about the past?" Kelly asked. "We, um …"

"We met your younger self yesterday, down in the tunnels that run below town," Emily finally blurted out. "I assume that, being known as a *bruja*, you know about and believe in the magic that exists in the tunnels, the time portal?"

Iris smiled, a slow upturning of her mouth. An almost dreamy look came into her eyes. "I am aware."

"When we visited you earlier, we mentioned Gabriel Graystone, but we didn't talk much about his personal life and death, about the torment he has suffered for a century now. We know about the stabbing, and that it was an accident," Emily said softly, her eyes filled with empathy for the restless ghost she had come to know. "He deserves peace, and so do you, Iris."

"Is there anything we can do now, to help Gabriel find peace?" Kelly asked, her expression kind. "It's just that he's … well, he's been pretty tormented."

Sam stepped forward. "Iris? Surely you know about this sort of thing …"

Iris hesitated, then spoke slowly. "There may be a way. We can perform a ritual to lay his spirit to rest."

"Then let's do it, please," Sam urged.

"Be very certain. It can be dangerous," Iris warned. They could see that her desire for redemption was balanced with concerns.

"Nothing worth doing is ever without risk," Emily replied. "Besides, we have our powerful artifacts to protect us."

"Very well," Iris agreed, her voice trembling slightly. Her gaze darted around the room. "But first, we need to gather a few things. Candles, herbs, crystals."

"Let's get started," Kelly said. "Tell us what to do."

Iris called for Sophie, who assisted her to stand. With the help of her cane, Iris led Sam, Kelly, and Emily to a small, dusty room toward the back of her home. Shelves in one corner held baskets of herbs and small boxes that were labeled in a spidery script. The old woman moved toward the organized clutter, her deeply veined hands hovering over various bottles and jars.

"Okay, so what do we do for this ritual?" Kelly asked. "I mean, besides the candles, herbs, and crystals?"

"First, we'll need to create a circle of protection," Iris explained, her voice wavering slightly as she spoke. "This will ensure that no malevolent spirits interfere with our efforts. Then, we'll invoke the spirits of justice and truth to guide us in our search for peace."

Sam's mind was already racing ahead to envision the ritual's steps. "And we can also use our own artifacts to strengthen the connection with Gabriel's spirit and give him rest, right?"

"Exactly," Iris confirmed, her commitment appearing stronger as she moved. "Samantha, please find the appropriate candles. Sophie can show you where I keep them. We want lavender for clarity and deep red ones for passion and justice."

Sam followed the caregiver to begin the task.

"Emily, go out into the garden. There, you will find the herbs."

Following Iris's instructions, Emily plucked fresh herbs – rosemary for remembrance, sage for wisdom, and thyme for courage. She carefully bundled them together, inhaling their earthy scents and hoping their combined power would help.

Meanwhile, Kelly rummaged through Iris's collection of crystals, searching for those that resonated with their intentions. She chose a smoky quartz to ground them during the ritual and a clear quartz to amplify their energies, as well as an amethyst for spiritual protection.

"Is this everything?" Sam asked, surveying the materials they had gathered. She held her carved wooden box in her hands, pulling energy from it, and she noticed Kelly doing the same.

"I know that box," Iris said, pointing, "the one with the cabochon stones."

Sam felt a rush of memories of the old woman who had insisted she take the box and use it for good purposes. She cleared her throat and asked the question again. "Iris, do we have everything for the ritual?"

Iris's dark eyes scanned over the items one last time. "Yes, I believe so. Bring all of these things and follow me."

Iris led Sam, Kelly, and Emily into another room, her movements cautious as she navigated the dimly lit space. The walls in here were adorned with antique tapestries depicting celestial beings and otherworldly landscapes, their colors faded with time. An old wooden table stood in the center of the space, its dark surface etched with arcane symbols. As the women moved about, lighting candles and placing them, the symbols seemed to shimmer as the flickering candlelight played upon them.

"This room has been in my family for generations. It's the oldest portion of my home," Iris said quietly, her voice barely above a whisper. "It's where we've always conducted our most important rituals." She made eye contact with Sam. "Your friend Bertha Martinez came here."

"The Graystones were not the ones using magic, were they?" Sam asked, the truth dawning on her.

Iris shook her head gently.

"Feels like we're stepping back in time," Kelly murmured, running her hand along the worn fabric of one of the tapestries.

Emily stood back, sending forth a little prayer, the hope of bringing peace to Gabriel's restless spirit. The candles flickered softly in the dimly lit room, casting shadows that seemed to echo the uncertainty they all felt.

"Let's get started," Sam urged. "Gabriel needs our help."

"Yes," Iris agreed, taking a deep breath to steady herself. "First, we need to cast the circle."

As they followed Iris's instructions, each woman took a chair at one of the cardinal points around the table. "We are forming a protective barrier between ourselves and any negative energies that might seek to interfere with our work," Iris said.

Sam lit more candles one by one, their warm glow casting an eerie ambiance over the ancient chamber.

"Okay," Emily said, focusing on the task at hand. "What's next?"

"Invocation," Iris replied, her gaze fixed on the flickering flames. "We must call upon the spirits to guide us in our quest for justice."

"Will they come?" Kelly asked, her voice tinged with uncertainty.

"They will if our intentions are pure," Iris assured her.

"Now, join hands and repeat after me."

Emily gave Kelly a quick glance. This was it. With their hands clasped together, the group began to chant in unison, the words resonating throughout the room.

"Please, spirits," Iris said, "help us bring justice to Gabriel's restless soul."

A gentle breeze wafted through the windowless room, then vanished.

As the last words of the invocation echoed through the chamber, silence descended upon the room, broken only by the steady crackling of herbs, which Iris sprinkled over the burning candles. The women found themselves holding their breath, waiting for some sign from the other side.

"Did it work?" Kelly whispered, her grip on Sam's hand tightening.

"Only time will tell," Iris replied, her eyes remaining fixed on the flickering candlelight. "But we've done our part. Now, it's up to the spirits to show us the way."

At once, the air in the room grew colder, and Sam could see her breath forming little clouds as she exhaled. A sense of dread filled her chest.

"Something's not right," Sam muttered, her voice barely audible over the sound of their own breathing. "It feels like we're being watched."

"Focus," Iris urged them. "Do not let anything distract you."

Kelly's hands began to tremble as she clutched tightly onto Sam and Emily. "Can you feel that?" she whispered, her eyes darting around the dimly lit room. "It's like … something ominous is here with us."

WHUMP!

The candles flickered wildly. Emily's heart raced.

"Keep your eyes on the candles and stay strong!" Iris shouted above the growing chaos. "We mustn't let malevolent forces interfere!"

A sudden gust of wind swept through the room, extinguishing the candles one by one. They sat in near darkness, but the connection between them remained unbroken.

"Do not fear," Iris instructed, her voice steady now. "Stay with it. Repeat my words."

She began chanting again, her voice steady despite the enveloping darkness. As they repeated her words, the oppressive atmosphere began to lift, replaced by a sense of calm.

And then, as suddenly as it had been extinguished, the candlelight returned, bathing the room in a warm, comforting glow. The air felt lighter, the dread vanishing in an instant.

"Look!" Kelly exclaimed, indicating a corner of the room where a faint apparition had materialized. It was the unmistakable figure of Gabriel, his eyes filled with gratitude and relief.

"Gabriel," Emily breathed, tears welling in her eyes. "We did it."

"Thank you," the ghostly figure whispered, his voice barely audible. "Thank you," Gabriel repeated, his form becoming a soft ethereal glow, hovering beside the group. His eyes seemed fixed on Iris.

"Goodbye, Gabriel," Emily murmured, wiping away tears.

"Happy travels, friend," Sam added.

"Take care," said Kelly.

As they watched, the ghostly figure slowly faded from sight, leaving an empty space that was quickly filled with an overwhelming sense of peace and resolution.

"Wow." Sam exhaled, still processing the surreal events that had just taken place.

Emily's voice sounded awestruck. "I can't believe we did it. We actually helped give peace to Gabriel's spirit."

Iris seemed exhausted as they all rose to leave the table. Sam called Sophie into the room to be sure the old woman didn't exert herself any further. They gathered their belongings and walked quietly toward the front door. There didn't seem to be much to say.

Chapter 45

The clouds broke apart and sun bathed the adobe buildings in a warm, golden glow as Emily, Samantha, and Kelly drove back into Taos. Sam called Sweet's Sweets to see if she was needed, but Jen and Becky both assured her things were quiet and they had it under control.

"Oh," Jen added. "The author you met the other day at Ivan's—she stopped in to see if you were here."

"Yes! Susan Slater. I'm sorry I missed her. She told me she was looking at property in the area."

"I told her you'd probably be in again tomorrow morning. I hope that was okay?"

"Absolutely. I'll check to see if I have her number, maybe give her a call."

But first, the trio had agreed they had one more errand. They had an obligation to the law, and the rest of their mission was not yet done.

Emily drove directly to the sheriff's office and parked out front. "How's your ankle, Sam? Would you be up for some more exploring?"

Sam rubbed the ankle, pleased at its miraculous healing. "I'm good. What do you have in mind?"

"Let's talk to Evan first. We promised to report to him once we knew who killed Gabriel."

"I hate this," Kelly said. "Turning Iris in."

"We're not really turning her in," Sam reminded. "But we do need to let him know Gabriel's death was an accident and how it happened, so he can close the case file. We'll do it as gently as possible."

They got out of the Jeep and stood for a moment, stretching their muscles after the bumpy ride down from Iris's house. Sam led the way and they found themselves in Evan's private office five minutes later.

The story spilled out, minus the details about traveling through time to the 1920s and speaking face-to-face with ghosts. Sam had thought about this all the way into town, how best to present it to law enforcement. She had decided, and briefed the others, that it would be best to tell the sheriff they'd come across documents that showed Gabriel involved with Iris Maxwell, and in a conversation with her she had described her own depression and how Gabriel had stopped her from suicide. When, or if, Evan questioned Iris, everything they told him was true and the stories would fit together. She didn't mention the ritual they'd just completed to free Gabriel's spirit and give him peace. Even in her own mind, that was just a bit woo-woo.

He had the case file on his desk, but asked very few questions, allowing Sam to act as spokesperson for the group. He made a few notes along the way, then closed the folder.

"What will happen to Iris?" Kelly asked. "She's *so* old now."

"I'm sure that will be taken into account," he said. "I'll need to interview her. If the story doesn't hold up, well … not sure, exactly. I'd need to confer with the prosecutor about the next steps."

Hopefully, for Gabriel's ghost himself, peace would be sufficient without seeing his former lover taken into a courtroom for the *justice* part of the equation.

Evan stood and the others followed suit. "Anything else you want to add?" he asked, noticing their hesitance to walk out.

"Actually," Emily inserted, "we need to get back into the Graystone mansion if that's possible."

He tilted his head, questioning.

"We told you that we'd brought out a box of documents, right? Well, some of those are what helped us to solve the case. Now, we'd like to go back and check for more. That family's history is such an important part of Taos … I'd like to catalogue everything and keep it with the research archives at the library."

Evan reached into the front pocket of his jeans and pulled something out. "I meant to return this to the real estate agent but never got over there. I don't suppose she'll squawk too bad if it takes me another day to do it."

He handed Emily the key,

"I will get this back to you tomorrow," she promised.

The women turned to leave. "Please go easy on Iris," Kelly begged. "She may be a little scary at first, but she's a good person."

With nothing more to accomplish there, the trio walked back out to Emily's Jeep, each of them knowing that there was no turning back. And as they left the sheriff's office, they all hoped the past had been put to rest and the future would go well, for all involved.

"It won't be dark for a couple more hours," Emily said, starting the Jeep. "Who's up for a trip to Graystone Manor?"

Chapter 46

I figured this would be a whole lot easier than making our way through the long labyrinth of tunnels," Emily said. "Not to mention, I'd rather know what's there now than to take the chance we'd come out sometime in the 1920s and have to confront a butler or somebody."

Kelly laughed. "Yeah, that could get awkward."

They pulled up in front of the magnificent stone house, parked where they had before, and retraced their steps through the house, heading downstairs with flashlights at the ready. This time, knowing their way around, they went directly to the small closet, removed each of the shelves, and activated the spring mechanism behind the baseboard. The hidden door opened with every bit as loud a screech as before.

"Gotta bring some WD40," Kelly muttered, rubbing

her ear.

Emily shone her light into the space, to be sure no surprises awaited, but it all appeared the same. The wooden boxes and trunks were still stacked neatly. Sam pointed out the Tiffany lamps she had admired the first time there, and the same moth-eaten sweaters were spilling out of the same trunk. Sam walked around, tapping the large floor stones with her flashlight.

"At least no one's been here to ransack the place," Kelly observed.

"So, if I were a treasure," Emily pondered, "where would I be hiding?"

She turned to look around at each of the four walls.

"Probably under something heavy," Kelly suggested. "Like that pile of steamer trunks in the corner."

"Okay, then. Let's go." Emily propped her flashlight on a table, with the beam aimed toward the stack of trunks.

She and Kelly lifted one piece of luggage after the other, setting them aside. When they got down to the stone floor, Sam came over and tapped it. "Nope. Just as solid as all the others," she said.

Kelly moved a Queen Anne chair aside and plopped down on it. "Give me just a second. You'd think I would be strong as a horse, after chasing a kid around all day."

Sam moved in and tapped the stone flooring where the chair had been. "No. No. N—Wait a second!"

Next to the chair was a table laden with lamps and dusty candles. Sam and Emily scooted it aside and Sam tapped the floor below.

"Ah-ha! This might be …"

Emily was looking around for something with which to pry at the large stones. A long-handled tool was propped up in the corner and she grabbed it. When she brought it near the place where Sam had detected the hollow sound, she noticed something more.

"Shine a light directly on that area," she requested, "Right on that one stone."

Sam complied and Emily spotted what looked like a broken chip in the stone, but on closer inspection she saw that it was a cutout place. And the tip of the tool in her hand had a prong that matched its size exactly.

"Let's see if we … ugh. Not easy."

All three of them got on it, putting some muscle to leverage the tool into the notch, twist it to the correct angle, and pry it upward. With a grating sound, the stone began to shift.

"I think if we swivel it slightly," Sam said, "it will push the stone to one side of whatever is below."

It worked. The stone inched aside, revealing a hole beneath. The three ladies lowered the heavy rock and rested it on the stable flooring beside it. Sam aimed a light into the hole and the others looked. The space below was not large—maybe two or three feet square, probably only a few inches deep. But what they saw took their breath away.

Gold. Stacks and stacks of gold bars.

Chapter 47

W hat on earth are we going to do?" Kelly whispered. Suddenly it seemed like a good idea to speak in low tones.

Sam seemed thoughtful. "Technically, I imagine it belongs to the house and if all contents are included with the sale of the place, whoever owns the house owns the gold."

"It's in foreclosure," Emily reminded. "So some bank owns it?"

"Or the person who comes along and buys the place," Sam said.

"Are we obligated to report this to the real estate agent?" Kelly stared into the hole once more.

"I don't know. I truly have no idea," Sam told them.

"I can look through some things in the library," Emily

said. "I seem to remember coming across documents that pertain to the ownership of found treasure. Maybe I can learn what the law is."

"Question is, the law now, or the law a hundred years ago?"

A shrug. "No idea." Emily looked back into the hole, counting. Ten gold bars were visible, with possibly more beneath those. According to the markings stamped into them, they dated back to the time when the Graystones lived here.

Sam spoke up. "I'd say, for now, we need to cover it back up and leave. We'll go home and think about it."

And so they did. Replacing the loose stone, they stacked trunks and furniture over the spot. Emily picked up the metal tool. "I'm taking this with me until we know what to do. As far as I'm concerned, this is Gabriel's inheritance and it should be his choice what happens to it. It wouldn't be impossible to open up that space without the special tool, but the odds are really slim that anyone would find the place and then be able to get into it."

Sam and Kelly nodded agreement with the plan.

The moon was rising in a twilight sky when they pulled up next to the library; Sam and Kelly headed to their own homes. No one would sleep that night.

* * *

Emily walked into the library and made a phone call. The conversation went to her liking, and she hung up with a smile and a better plan to organize the contents of this wonderful little business she'd inherited. She would begin with the documents that related to Gabriel Graystone.

Picking up his diary and his brother's letters, she grabbed a pack of index cards then locked up and walked across the patio to her house.

She realized she was hungry but a search of the fridge didn't show her anything she wanted.

"Remember when I always kept the cookie jar full for you?" Valerie's voice startled her.

Emily turned toward the sound and smiled. "I do. You always made my summers here in Taos very special."

"And now someone else has made your days special ..."

Emily blushed a little.

"... hasn't he?"

"Thinking of Gabriel makes me a little bit sad. Such a good man, one whose life ended much too soon."

Valerie nodded. "It happens."

"Could we bake cookies again?"

"You'll have to do all the work," the ghost said with a chuckle.

"Tell me what to do."

Fifteen minutes later the first batch was in the oven, delicate butter cookies, since Em had no chocolate or nuts or raisins on hand. When they came out, she placed a second sheet in the oven and then scooped up three of the warm ones and placed them on a napkin.

"What's really on your mind?" Valerie asked. "I know you're thinking of more than the special man who tried to capture your heart."

She floated over to the table where Emily had set a cup of tea and her cookies. "Wait—don't tell me. I think you have a special project on your mind."

Emily patted the stack of letters she'd brought home with her.

"Not only those," Valerie said, her eyes betraying their wisdom. "It's something more, something bigger."

Emily let the first butter cookie dissolve in her mouth, then savored a long sip of the tea to go with it. "Maybe."

"You know … there is a bit of money in the Plankhurst Trust. It's not a great fortune, but I know your grandfather would be pleased if you chose to support a worthy local cause of some kind."

"Is that a hint?" Emily asked, turning her head.

The oven timer went off just then and she jumped up to pull out the cookie sheet before they could over-brown. When she turned back around, Valerie was gone.

"Yeah, right. Duck out on me just when I have questions!"

But there was no response. Emily sighed and set about cleaning up the kitchen. When Valerie still had not appeared, Em refreshed her tea mug and carried it to the living room, along with the items she'd brought home from the library. She thought of calling out to Gabriel, but paused. His spirit was at peace, finally. She should leave him alone. She could surely find the answers to her questions among the family papers.

Chapter 48

The next morning, Sam picked up a cup and carefully measured amaretto for her top-secret cheesecake recipe. She had never let anyone but Julio make that one, as it was one of her bestselling items. She set the bottle back on the shelf at the same time she heard animated voices out front.

"Sounds like Emily," Becky said, from where she had six wedding cake tiers laid out for assembly.

"I think you're right." Sam turned the rest of the cheesecake recipe over to Julio and walked to the front, wiping her hands on a clean towel.

Emily raised an eyebrow when Sam greeted her. "I promised Evan I'd return that key today, but I stopped in to see if you and Kelly want to come along. I have a feeling he'll let us know what he decided to do about Iris and the confession."

"You're probably right. Kelly's tied up at home, but let me …"

Jen spoke up. "Sam, just go if you need to. We'll manage for a while here."

"Hopefully it won't take more than fifteen or twenty minutes," Emily said. "I have another appointment at ten."

"Really?"

But Em didn't pick up the hint. She rushed out to her Jeep, leaving Sam to follow. She was rummaging in her purse when Sam took her seat and buckled the seatbelt.

"Just checking to be sure I brought the key with me," Emily said. She held it up, dropped it in the cup holder, and backed out.

Less than three minutes later they were at the sheriff's department.

"Sam, Emily," Evan Richards greeted them as they entered his office.

Sam tried to read his expression and couldn't.

"I've been going over all the evidence and thinking about Iris's situation."

"And?" Sam asked cautiously, her expression a mix of hope and concern.

"Given her age and status in our community, I don't think it's right to prosecute her," he said quietly, looking at the two women before him. "She's lived a long life, and if she did have any involvement in Gabriel's death, it was more than a century ago."

"Thank you, Evan," Sam exhaled in relief, feeling a warmth spread through her chest. "It's the right decision."

"Good," Sheriff Richards said, satisfied with their response. "I'm glad you agree. Even though she probably would have been charged with something back in the day, it's been too long. Can you imagine the stink I'd cause by arresting the state's oldest living citizen?"

"Oh, definitely," Emily chimed in, grateful for the news. "Iris doesn't have a lot of fight left in her. It's time to just let her live out her remaining days in peace."

Sam and Emily left the office, exchanging relieved glances as they stepped outside. The burden of guilt had been lifted from their hearts, knowing they'd done their duty by reporting their findings, and equally knowing they were not responsible for sending an old woman to trial.

"It's good news, all the way around," Emily said as she drove Sam back to the bakery. "Gabriel's at peace, Iris can be at peace, I hope. And I think we all feel better too."

"Want to come in for a coffee? Blueberry scone, on the house …?"

"Would love to but I can't."

"Ah, right. Your other appointment." Sam waited a long enough moment but clearly Emily wasn't going to share details. Which was fine. Even in a small town, not everything was everybody's business.

A bright red Mini-Cooper with white stripes pulled into the lot beside Emily's Jeep. Sam realized the driver was Susan Slater, the author.

"Sam! So glad I caught you," Susan called out. "Ivan wants me to sign some more books, and I simply *had* to come by for more of your pumpkin cheesecake. I hope there's some left?"

"Hi, Susan, come on in." Sam found her smile matching the ready friendliness of the other woman.

Jen saw them coming. "Pumpkin cheesecake? I saved you two slices."

"Wonderful. One for here, with some of that fabulous

coffee of yours, and one to take home." Susan turned to Sam. "Do you have a moment to join me? I'm on my way back to Albuquerque …"

"Sure. Grab that table, and I'll just check in with the kitchen. Two seconds."

When she returned, her new friend was sticking a fork into her slice of cheesecake. Her eyes rolled upward as she took the first bite. "Ummm … heaven."

"You chose the right time of year to be here," Sam said, pouring herself a mug of her signature blend coffee. "We only make the pumpkin flavor in the fall. If it's out of the oven in time, I'm going to send you home with a slice of the amaretto. Now *that* one gets raves all year."

Susan laughed and picked up her mug.

"So, you told me you'd been looking at property around town, right? It would be great to have you here as a neighbor, and I know Ivan would love hosting a famous author much more frequently. How's the search going?"

Susan gave an enigmatic smile. "I'm not sure if this is the place for me or not. But anything's possible."

Sam smiled back. Small town life, after living in a city, could take some adjustment. "But you are still writing your Ben Pecos mystery series, aren't you?"

"Oh, definitely. Ben is a fixture. Got the whole tall, dark, and handsome thing going for him. I suspect most of *my* fans are actually Ben's fans."

Sam laughed. "Could be. I know Ivan's book club members are definitely sold."

"Speaking of which …" Susan said, scraping the last of her cheesecake from the plate. "I need to get over there and sign his stock and then hit the road. Sam, it's been great fun, and you know I'll be back in here, anytime I come to Taos."

They stood and hugged. Sam saw her to the door, wondering when that next visit might take place. She walked back to the kitchen, pulling out her phone to inform Kelly about the sheriff's decision on Iris Maxwell's confession.

Chapter 49

Emily blew dust off the spine of a book, set it aside, and picked up the neat stack of index cards she'd finished compiling. The history of the Maldonado family was not complete, not by any means, but she'd dedicated two days to organizing the information she had so far.

Since the encounter in the tunnel, where Augustine and Antonio threatened them and the ladies reported it to the sheriff of the past, Em had wondered whether Sheriff Fineman ever captured the Maldonado brothers and locked them away. The question lingered, the fact that she and Kelly might have changed history by their actions.

She'd been unable to find anything in the news archives to indicate that the brothers had gone to prison around 1920. She reached across her worktable and picked up the crackling old newspaper she'd taken from the wall outside the speakeasy, the account of their arrest on suspicion of a string of robberies.

"No," she murmured, shaking her head, "I think you two kept getting away with things. I'll even bet that when I get the chance to research the old news sources in Santa Fe, I imagine you went there and disrupted the political scene. If Sheriff Fineman had been able to make a serious crime stick, and if you'd gone to prison, these later articles would have never been written."

She set the clipping down and sighed. A sound outside the window attracted her attention, and she looked up to see a car pulling into the tiny parking lot out front. She stood and went to the door to let her visitor in.

"Kelly! Hey, I didn't know you were coming over."

Kelly laughed, her cinnamon curls shaking as she walked in. "Actually, I didn't either. I dropped Ana off to bake cookies with Mom, and had to see how you're doing."

Emily waved a hand toward the messy table. "Better than you'd guess by looking at this."

"I keep thinking about what we discovered at the mansion, the um …"

"Gold? It's okay. There's no one around to hear you say it."

"I can't seem to let go of the idea that it'll stay sealed up in that secret room in the basement, and when someone buys the place they'll either find it or they won't, but they'll never know where it came from or the facts surrounding Gabriel's life and death."

Emily nodded thoughtfully.

"Do you think we should go back? Maybe take it someplace for safe keeping?" Kelly asked. She paced to the end of the room and held up both hands. "Okay, I know. It's not ours to take. I need to forget about it."

"We'll see. Things tend to work out. Meanwhile, I've been indexing and cross-referencing the Maldonado history and am about to start with the Graystones. Want to stay and help?"

"Sure. But don't let me get totally lost in this. Mom will want a reprieve from Ana after an hour or two."

Emily pointed her to a stack of letters and explained her manner of creating an index card as a cross-reference to the events of the time. Eventually, she would put it all on her computer. Kelly sat on one side of the table, Emily on the other, reading through documents.

Fifteen minutes later, Emily's gasp got Kelly's attention. "I had always wondered what ever happened to Clara Maldonado," she said, her eyes wide. "Here's a letter from her mother to an aunt in Albuquerque. It looks like after Gabriel died she went into a convent, at age nineteen, and never spoke of the events that happened. The letter is dated 1955, so Clara would have reached middle age by then."

"Wow, a convent. So Gabriel really was the love of her life."

"Sounds like she never wanted anything else for herself after he was gone."

"So sad."

"It was," Emily agreed.

They worked in silence, each with a set of documents, until the old clock on the shelf chimed.

Kelly stood. "This has been so interesting, but I really should go."

"One of these days I want to get back over to the mansion and see if there are any documents we might have missed," Emily told her. "I feel like I'm on a roll here, getting this material organized finally. And it would be a real shame if a new owner went through the Graystones' things and tossed out papers because they didn't think they were important."

"That would be terrible. Yes, absolutely. Count me in."

Chapter 50

Sam walked Ana and Kelly out to their car, placing a bakery box of frosted cookies on Ana's lap.

"I'm saving these for when my daddy comes home," Ana said with a wide smile. "He always loves our cookies. And I made a picture for Auntie Emily." She handed a folded sheet of paper to Kelly.

"What's this? It looks like a fancy room with a big Christmas tree?"

Ana just smiled. "She'll know."

"It's *really* well done, honey. And you had time to bake cookies, which I suspect you've already eaten more than your share during the afternoon," Kelly told her little daughter. "We'll put these in the freezer and they'll be great in a few days."

"So, what did you do with your free afternoon?" Sam

asked as Kelly got in and buckled her seatbelt.

"Helped Emily catalog more of the Graystone family documents. We're thinking we might go back at some point and see if there's anything we missed at the last visit."

Sam merely smiled, not wanting to say the word *treasure* in front of her granddaughter. You never knew what kids would repeat. She patted the top of the car as Kelly put it in gear. "Be safe," she said.

Back in the kitchen at Sweet's Sweets, Becky already had the worktable cleaned up. Baking sessions with Ana tended to be a bit lavish with clouds of flour and spatters of icing.

"What's on the schedule for the rest of the week?" Sam asked, picking up the stack of orders.

"Mostly birthdays. Only two weddings, and we have a couple days to get those ready."

Sam surveyed the shelf where they stored their flavorings and certain staple items. "Looks like everything's under control here. I'm going to make a run to the supermarket and then go home. Beau hasn't seen a lot of me in recent days, and I thought I'd cook his favorite barbeque ribs tonight."

Becky assured her everything would be fine at the bakery. "Go. The ribs sound wonderful."

Ten minutes later, Sam was staring at the shelves, trying to spot the brand of barbeque sauce she usually bought, when she sensed someone trying to push their cart past. She straightened, ready to apologize for being in the way, when she recognized the person.

"Annette?"

The woman's head popped up.

"Samantha Sweet. I came by your house …"

"I remember." Her face remained rigid, unsmiling.

"Look, I wanted to … I mean, I tried calling and coming by. I want to apologize if I said or did something that offended your family. I've been involved in helping with some historical research, but I didn't mean to besmirch the Maldonado name."

Annette softened, but only a little.

"Any connection between Augustine and Antonio Maldonado and the Graystone murder … well, they weren't connected in the way we originally thought."

A vision flashed before her, of the way the two men confronted her in the tunnels, their aggressive manner and the fact that they'd committed other crimes, later. But now was not the time to bring that up.

"Annette, there were certain things they did, but their misdeeds and crimes happened a hundred years ago. Nothing that's relevant now. Please don't think I was making accusations—"

Annette suddenly got busy studying the items in her shopping cart.

"Look, what I'm saying is that the past is past." Images from certain parts of history flashed by Sam. "The past is past, and no one today should be shamed or blamed or take on something their ancestors did. Not yours, not mine, not anyone's. Blaming accomplishes nothing. Harboring guilt serves no purpose. We all have skeletons in the closet, things we'd rather did not exist. But we live now, in the present time. We can't let those dark times taint our friendships and our enjoyment of life today."

When she looked back up, Annette had tears in her eyes. "Thank you. I agree."

"Can we have a friendship now and just leave the past out of it?"

The woman reached out and touched Sam's hand, and Sam clasped hers in return. "Be well, my dear."

Chapter 51

The next morning, Sam was placing trays of scones and muffins in the display case when the phone rang. Jen picked it up.

"It's Evan Richards," she said.

"I'll grab it in the kitchen," Sam told her, eyeing the full tables and noisy crowd in the sales room.

Wiping her hands on her apron, she walked to her desk and picked up the receiver. "Hey, Evan."

"Just wanted to let you know, Iris Maxwell passed away last night, Sam," Sheriff Richards' solemn voice informed her. "In her sleep."

Sam felt a pang in her heart as the news sank in. "Oh, Evan, I'm so sorry," she murmured.

"Me too," he replied softly. "She lived a long life, and at least she died peacefully. It's all we could've hoped for."

"True," she agreed, wondering what other secrets might still exist in Iris's past, deciding they could remain buried.

As Sam placed the phone back on its cradle, she couldn't help but feel a sense of loss for the woman who had been such an enigma. Despite her age and her confession about Gabriel's death, there was a melancholy air to her passing that left Sam feeling unsettled.

The back door opened and Kelly walked in. She took one look at Sam and stopped. "Mom? Everything okay?"

"Fine, just received some sad news," Sam replied, making an effort to keep her voice steady as she told Kelly.

"We should let Emily know." Kelly pulled out her phone and made the call.

"Will there be a funeral?" Emily asked. "We should go, and send some flowers."

Sam looked up. "I forgot to ask. I'll call Sophie and find out."

The caregiver's voice sounded sad when she told Sam that Iris really had no friends and hadn't wanted a traditional service. "She asked to be cremated and have her ashes scattered here on her property."

"We can't let her life go entirely unnoticed," Sam said. "We'll plan something."

* * *

A week passed before Sophie called to say she had picked up Iris's ashes from the funeral director.

"When would you like to do this?" Sam asked gently.

They agreed to meet that afternoon just before sunset, so Emily, Kelly, and Sam made the drive up the rocky hillside once again. Thin clouds wisped across the orange sky, creating layers of red, pink, and magenta, vivid against the black silhouette of the volcanos in the distance. It was a perfect example of a New Mexico sunset, and exactly the right setting to say goodbye to Iris.

From a bamboo box, Sophie pulled the sealed plastic bag containing the cremains, and they faced the western horizon as she opened the bag and let the gentle easterly breeze carry the contents over the land Iris had loved so much.

As the light began to fade, they made their way back to the house. Sophie lit several lamps and turned toward the others.

"Emily, Iris left a very simple list of her final wishes. She wanted you to have anything you would like, in the way of documents, diaries and such, for your library."

"Oh my, that's *so* generous." Emily's voice cracked.

Sophie handed a single sheet of paper to Sam, who read it and then looked up. "She wanted you to have her house, to stay here and take care of it, Sophie."

Sophie nodded. "I've been with her for more than ten years, and she knew how much I'd come to love this little place."

"I think it's very fitting," Sam said, giving her a hug.

"We're all going over to Sweet's Sweets," Kelly said. "Please come along. A few friends wanted to pay their respects, so we'll serve coffee and pastries, and everyone can share their memories of this interesting woman who had such an amazingly long life."

Chapter 52

By eight p.m. when everyone gathered at the bakery, Sam had put together a huge assortment of sweets and savories—hot quiches, sausage stuffed rolls, and green chile cheese breads, along with three flavors of cheesecake, mini-cinnamon rolls, brownies, lemon bars, and pumpkin cookies. Her signature coffee accompanied herbal teas, black teas, and hot chocolate.

Evan and Rico represented the sheriff's department, and even the mayor showed up, not wanting to miss an opportunity to say a few words about the loss of the state's oldest citizen—a few words that turned into a fifteen-minute speech.

Friends who hadn't even known Iris came, showing their support for Emily, for Sam's family, and for Sophie. Zoë and Darryl, Evan's wife and Kelly's friend, Riki, and even Annette Maldonado and her husband came. Sam was glad they'd had the chance to clear the air about the past so everyone felt comfortable.

As they asked anyone with a memory of Iris to share, it seemed few had known her, but Annette Maldonado stepped up.

"My mother was a friend of Iris's," she said, "and I remember times when I was a child and I would linger at the edge of the room while the two of them gossiped and brewed things on the stove. Some said Iris was a *bruja*, but I got the impression she was more likely a *curandera*, a healer. She had ways with herbs and plants. She could cure my childhood colds and make poultices for my brothers' scrapes and cuts. And I suspect she and my mother added 'a little something' to their tea at times because they could get quite silly after sharing a pot of it."

Annette blushed a little and sat down. Sophie shared memories of how much energy Iris had, even in recent months, and expressed happiness that her friend and employer had enjoyed robust health.

"Maybe she was still brewing those special teas," she said with a mischievous glance at Annette.

The stories petered out and guests began to head for the door. Sam made certain everyone took home some of the goodies. Evan touched Sam's elbow as Riki chose a few treats and Kelly put them into a bag.

"Got some more news, right before I left to come over here," he said to Sam, his voice low. "The real estate agent stopped by for the key to the Graystone property. She's had an offer on it, and it looks like the deal will go through, she told me."

"I'll pass that along." Sam felt a pang of regret that

they'd never gone back over to check for more Graystone documents.

When, at last, they were alone, she told Emily and Kelly what Evan had said.

"I'll find a way to make sure the historic items aren't tossed out in the trash," Emily assured her. "I tell you, I've come across so many interesting things while cataloguing the library contents … I could keep us all busy with mysteries to solve for a good long time."

"As long as it doesn't involve going down into those tunnels a whole lot more," Kelly said, her eyes wide.

"There's another bit of news," Emily told them. "Rico solved the question of who tried to break into the library."

"Really—that's great!" Kelly said. "Did he say who it was, and why?"

A smile played on Emily's face. "Some young guy who's been caught before, breaking into places at night. Rico picked him up trying to get into the public library last night."

"A library thief?" Sam's face registered skepticism.

"You'll howl when you hear this. Apparently, the kid watched some video where it was stated that, quote, 'Libraries have long held the riches of civilization.' He took it to mean actual money, and thought he could just break in and find a bundle of cash."

They all got a good laugh over the story as they began to put away the party leftovers. But then the mood turned serious again.

"Iris's death just doesn't feel real," Emily murmured, rubbing her temples. "She was like a force of nature."

"A hundred twenty years old," Kelly said softly, shaking her head in disbelief. "She lived through so much history.

I wonder how much more she knew. Things we never discovered."

"Probably a great deal. Can you imagine the experiences and memories a person would accumulate in that amount of time?" Sam replied, feeling a pang of regret for not having asked Iris more questions when they had the chance. She wished she'd had more opportunities to talk with her, perhaps to discover more about her experiences as a *bruja* or to know whether those tales were more rumor than fact.

"Here's to Iris," Emily murmured, raising her teacup in tribute. "May she rest in peace."

"Here's to Iris," the others echoed.

They were quiet for several minutes, each lost in her own thoughts, until Kelly piped up. "I can't help thinking about the gold that's hidden under the floor at the Graystone place. We never did get the chance to go back and get it—*if* that's what we'd decided to do."

Emily shifted in her seat, looking a little embarrassed. "So ... I mentioned that I'll make sure nothing from Graystone Manor gets thrown away, and the way I know that's going to happen is because ..."

She paused and met their eyes. "I'm the one who bought the place. In a couple more weeks, it will be signed and sealed, and I'll be the proud owner of a very strangely renovated, pieced-together slice of Taos history."

"What! Oh my gosh, Em. What will you do with it?" Kelly asked, staring.

An enigmatic smile lit up her face. "You'll have to wait and see."

Epilogue

Snow began falling in gentle flakes on December first, the day the envelopes arrived. Sam received one at the bakery; Kelly's came to the mailbox in front of her lovely Victorian home. Jen was looking on when Sam pulled out the engraved card and read it aloud:

You are invited to attend a gala celebration of 19th Century Taos History at Graystone Manor. December 15th, 8 p.m. Champagne and hors d'oeuvres and a tour of the historic home. Friends and family welcome. Please RSVP to Emily Plankhurst.

Emily was purposely evasive when Sam called and asked questions. "Just bring your crew from the bakery, if they're interested, and of course Beau should come too."

The fact that she placed an order from Sweet's Sweets for eight dozen assorted bite-sized desserts told Sam she was expecting a big turnout. Sam shared the news with everyone and they set to work planning the selection of sweets and ordering the ingredients.

Kelly called as Sam was finalizing her list. "Ana is beside herself with excitement. She knows she'll get a new party dress, since she's outgrown everything from last year's holiday season. And Scott is even looking forward to it. He's put the finishing touches on his latest Maddie Plimpton mystery for kids, and he's ready to celebrate."

"I hadn't heard from Emily in weeks," Sam said. "Now we know what she's been doing with her time."

"I wonder … Do you suppose she's planning to move into the mansion?"

"I wouldn't think so—she loves living in her grandparents' home and being handy to the library. Plus, could you imagine one person rattling around in that huge old place?"

They discussed it, and the upcoming party, without coming to any conclusions, until Sam realized she needed to get busy with her regular slew of holiday orders.

* * *

December fifteenth dawned as one of those cold, crisp winter days. A couple inches of snow had fallen earlier in the week, but most of it was gone and there was none in today's forecast, so Sam felt some relief that no one would encounter difficulties in driving out to the Graystone place.

"I wonder if we're supposed to start calling it the Plankhurst Mansion now?" she mused, as she and Beau dressed that evening.

Sam had opted for silky black slacks and a silver sparkly tunic. For dressy occasions, Beau always defaulted to his dark Western suit of fine wool, with yokes on the jacket. His concession to the fact that it was nearly Christmas, was his string tie with a gleaming malachite stone as the centerpiece. There would be men in tuxedos at the event, Sam felt sure, but Beau would outclass them all.

She had delivered the desserts to the mansion earlier in the day, but aside from a crew of six who were decorating a twenty-foot-tall Christmas tree in the foyer and some other signs of pre-party bustle, Emily refused to divulge much else. She'd quickly handed off the bakery boxes to a helper, with instructions to take them to the kitchen, and subtly walked Sam back out to her van before she could snoop.

They arrived at 8:05, expecting to be a bit early, but Sam was surprised to see more than a dozen cars already parked and more arriving behind them. Valets in black down jackets directed each vehicle to drive under the portico (which Sam would swear had a new coat of paint on the trim), and others met them to open their doors and show them to the front door.

When they walked in, Sam's hand tucked into Beau's elbow, she caught her breath. The foyer was lit by the ornate Christmas tree and soft lights amid greenery on the stair railing. The overhead chandelier sparkled with a recent cleaning, and the marble floor gleamed beneath. Soft jazzy music drifted from somewhere nearby, as guests mingled into the formal parlor and dining room. The plain white walls had been painted and papered in appropriate colors from the early 1900s.

"Wow. Not at all like it looked three months ago,"

she said under her breath to Beau. But, in fact, there was something eerily familiar about the scene.

Emily's chipper voice rose above the background sounds as she greeted them. Someone offered to take their coats, and a waiter with a tray of champagne flutes circulated.

"There's a full bar set up in the dining room, if you'd prefer something else," Emily told them. "Come in, mingle, have something to eat—there's plenty."

"Em, it's … it's just amazing," Sam told her. "Even a quick glimpse of the other rooms … I mean, you've made miraculous changes here."

A gust of cool air told them of new arrivals, and they looked around to see that Kelly, Scott, and Ana had entered.

"Oh. My. Gosh," Kelly said. "This is—"

"Just the way I drew it," Ana whispered.

Emily laughed with delight. "I'm so glad you like it. You two are the only ones, really, who saw it the way it was before."

"How did you—? This is just *so* much better. So much more authentic." Kelly's glance went everywhere at once.

Emily pulled them to the far end of the foyer where it was less crowded, while the men went off in search of a bourbon. "We'll be giving a little tour later," she told them. "This was such a labor of love, and it's been so much fun putting it together."

"I have to ask … how did you do it so quickly?" Sam looked around at the furnishings, the artwork on the walls, the rugs and wallpapers. She thought of her carved box and the number of times its power had helped her to accomplish huge tasks quickly, but Emily didn't have that.

"Lots of help and plenty of money to work with. I've

used part of the gold for the renovations, part of it to set up a foundation to fund museum operations into the future." Emily stared at the floor for a second, her cheeks turning pink. "And then there were some inside tips."

"Gabriel? He's come back and visited you again?"

Em gave a big grin. "Once I took possession of the place, I remembered the things Iris had us do that day at her house. I performed a cleansing ritual on the whole house before doing anything else. Once Gabriel felt comfortable here, he came back. We explored a little, and he showed me where the old tunnel entrance was. It is—I think, fortunately—now collapsed and inaccessible.

"He also showed me two attic rooms that had been walled off, spaces full of items that had belonged to his family. Much of the furniture I've used in the rooms was theirs. And the rest—people have been so generous in coming up with things and donating them."

"Oh, Em, that's fantastic!" Kelly told her. "Is Gabriel—is he still around?"

"Well … maybe … He doesn't care for crowds much."

A woman in a long blue dress approached and touched Emily's arm, whispering something to her.

"I need to see someone," Emily apologized to Sam and Kelly. "Please, walk around and look at the place, get some food, and mingle. I'll be conducting a little tour once everyone has settled in."

She rushed to the front door to greet a new arrival. Sam recognized the mayor and his wife, and she was fairly sure it was their State Senator accompanying them.

"Shall we find our husbands and take a look at the other rooms?" Kelly asked.

They located Beau and Scott approximately where they

expected to, standing near the laden buffet table, chatting with Zoë and Darryl, plates of queso dip and chips in hand.

"… worked out great," Darryl was saying. "When Emily called in September, we'd just finished a house in town and I was looking for the next project." He waved a hand around the dining room. "And this was it. Biggest trick was finding period-appropriate wallpaper and getting it here in time. I tell you, that Emily is a wonder at locating stuff like that. Would you believe, my decorator was papering this room the day before yesterday? The minute she was out of here, the guys painted the trim and moved the furniture in."

Sam gave him a light punch on the arm. "And you didn't think to tell me about all this?"

"Sworn to secrecy," he said. "Plus, there was not a spare minute. We worked dawn to dark, sometimes later, every day of the week."

"Well done. I can't imagine." Kelly took a chip from Scott's plate and swiped in into the cheese dip. She turned to her husband. "Where's our daughter?"

"Staring at the Christmas tree. She's never seen one so tall. I told her to look but not touch. And just to be sure, I can see her through the doorway. She's fine."

The ding-ding-ding of cutlery against glass got their attention and everyone stopped talking. From the foyer came Emily's voice. Guests drifted from the parlor and dining room to see her, standing on the stairs a couple of feet above the crowd.

"First, I'd like to welcome everyone and to thank all of you for your generous help in getting this whole project put together. Tonight's celebration is to announce the opening of the newest historic site in Taos, the Graystone Manor

Museum. Our purpose is to showcase what a vibrant town Taos was at the end of the nineteenth and beginning of the twentieth century. Long before New Mexico became a state, in 1912, there were thriving communities here. Many aspects of our culture—Indian and Spanish, in particular—are highlighted in other museums around town.

"But two prominent families—the Graystones and the Maldonados—received little attention beyond the time when they were here. Active in land development, mining, and business, both families moved on to other endeavors. But their time in Taos was important and should be remembered.

"With seed money from the Plankhurst Trust, I was able to purchase Graystone Manor for the purpose of restoring it to its glory days and making it available so residents and visitors could tour the home and learn more about this time in our history. The early 1900s saw the art community bloom here, and Gabriel Graystone was a budding artist who never lived long enough to make a career of his talent. His father had bigger plans, of a political nature, but those were thwarted as well when he died so young.

"Anyway, I'm not going to fill your evening with the entire history of the family and their contemporaries. For anyone interested, I'd like to show you around the house a bit, to show you the rooms we've restored so far. There is much yet to be done, as you will see. Anyone who knew my grandparents is well aware that the Plankhursts are avid history buffs, and we are always looking for more to share, more documentation on the history of our area. It's through the donation of documents and items that we've been able to create what we have here. Several of the paintings were done by young Gabriel Graystone himself, including an unfinished piece upstairs in what would have been his studio.

"Governor Sanchez—my personal thanks to you for giving us access to items from the Graystone home in Santa Fe, where the family moved and established political prominence after leaving Taos." She gave a nod to the puffed-up politician.

"Just quickly—special thanks go out to Annette and Jaime Maldonado for giving us enough personal items from the Maldonado family that we were able to create one exhibit entitled Prominent Taos Families. We're adding to it, all the time." A quick round of applause erupted, causing Annette to blush furiously. "Graystone Manor Museum will be run by a board of directors, and I'm pleased to say several of them are also prominent with the various historical preservation groups in the state, *and* we can boast several from the art preservation groups that help us keep everything in our little museum authentic. Thank you, all of you, *so* very much. We could not have done this without you." She gave a little bow toward the crowd.

"And, finally, I'd be remiss if I didn't give a shout-out to Darryl Chartrain, contractor extraordinaire who pulled off an amazing amount of structural and decorative refurbishments in an incredibly short time. We would not be hosting such a fine party tonight if not for his crew."

She pointed toward Darryl and began the wave of applause that quickly filled the room.

"And to Miss Anastasia Porter who provided a vision of this foyer and the party." Ana held out the skirts of her pretty dress and dropped a neat curtsy for the crowd.

"And now, our docents in training will be happy to show you around. Let's say twenty people or so, at a time.

And everyone, please keep working on the food and drinks. There's a lot!"

The docents, who Sam now recognized as the young women in the long blue dresses and men in matching blue shirts, stepped forward. Emily, flushed with the success of her speech, stepped aside so the first group could ascend the stairs. She spotted Sam and Kelly in the dining room doorway and headed toward them.

"I feel like I've said *amazing* about a hundred times tonight," Kelly told her. "But it's true."

Emily hooked her arms through theirs. "Come to the kitchen a minute." She led the way past the catering crew who were mostly in the clean-up phase of their job, heading for the butler's pantry. "I need to give you both an extra huge thanks, and it's best done in a quiet spot. Gabriel didn't want his presence revealed to the crowd."

"Gabriel's—?" Kelly stared as a faintly transparent man in a long duster and wide-brimmed hat walked into the pantry from the adjoining storage cupboard.

Emily stepped toward him, her face glowing. "Without the three of you, none of this would have been possible. Sam and Kelly, you didn't question, you didn't call me crazy, you just pitched in and helped solve the mystery. Gabriel, you gave me a purpose, the task of finding the truth about your life."

His ghost smiled warmly. "And you did, admirably so, Emily. Samantha. Kelly. All of you. I am indebted."

Emily looked into his eyes. "You have your home back, Gabriel. Rather than hanging out in the dark of the tunnels or the misty road on Bent Street, this is your home, your place to rest, to paint, whatever it is a ghost likes to do. There will be spaces here where you need not fear anyone will turn you away."

She turned to the others with a wink. "I would swear that the unfinished painting in the upstairs studio is becoming a little more finished each day."

Sam and Kelly watched as Gabriel leaned forward, placed a gentle kiss on Emily's cheek, and his image faded away.

Author's Note

From the moment I knew I would put a ghost in this story, I wanted to know whether Taos has any history of haunted places. Sightings of ghostly horses, soldiers, and other people along Bent Street are told by many. Same with accounts of people who've seen frightening apparitions near the many roadside *descansos* in the area. But my imagination really revved up when I learned that there actually are tunnels beneath the town of Taos. In researching them, I found several references, mainly described as Emily first saw them, with rickety supports and crumbling walls. I've not seen these tunnels myself, and I have no idea how extensive they were at one time. The descriptions I've included here involve pure imagination and lots of artistic license.

On a poignant note, I lost a dear friend this year, fellow

mystery author Susan Slater. Among the outpouring of love and kindness that I received from my readers, one suggestion spoke to my heart. Thank you, Martha Miller, who suggested I could include Susan in my next book, as a visiting author at Ivan's bookshop. I can so clearly hear Susan's voice in my head, to this day, and I think I've captured it in the conversations she has with Sam here. Susan still shows up regularly in my dreams, so maybe she will come back in another book sometime.

Another special thank-you goes out to my good friend Kathy Castellanos of Hermosillo, Mexico, who graciously allowed the use of her name as the art supply shop owner in this story. You create the most fun, whimsical, and delightful watercolors, and I have kept every one you've ever sent me. Love you, *mi amiga*!

In the spirit of begging forgiveness, please pardon the liberties I've taken with the *Taos News*, where back issues are only archived from 1959 onward. The original newspaper in town, which would have been around in Gabriel's time, was *El Crepusculo,* the predecessor of the current paper.

Finally, always, always … my eternal thanks go to my editor, Stephanie Dewey, and her dream team of beta readers (Marcia Koopmann, Susan Gross, Amy Connolley, Brooke Baxter, Dawn Hasiotis, Georgia Ryle, Eve Osborne, and Donna Townsend) for their usual expertise at catching all those boo-boos that I can't seem to spot on my own. All of you help to put the polish on the finished books, and I so appreciate it. To Dan and Daisy and to all of you, my readers, who add the bright spots to all my days!

Connie

Get another Connie Shelton book—FREE! <u>Click here to find out how</u>

Thank you for taking the time to read *Haunted Sweets*. If you enjoyed it, please consider telling your friends or posting a short review. Word of mouth is an author's best friend and is much appreciated.
Thank you,
Connie Shelton

There's more coming for Samantha and family!
In the meantime, if you've missed any…
Scan the QR code to get the links to all of them.

Sign up for Connie Shelton's free mystery newsletter at www.connieshelton.com
and receive advance information about new books, along with a chance at prizes, discounts and other mystery news!

Contact by email: connie@connieshelton.com
Follow Connie Shelton on Twitter, Pinterest and Facebook

Books by Connie Shelton

The Charlie Parker Series
Deadly Gamble
Vacations Can Be Murder
Partnerships Can Be Murder
Small Towns Can Be Murder
Memories Can Be Murder
Honeymoons Can Be Murder
Reunions Can Be Murder
Competition Can Be Murder
Balloons Can Be Murder
Obsessions Can Be Murder
Gossip Can Be Murder
Stardom Can Be Murder
Phantoms Can Be Murder
Buried Secrets Can Be Murder
Legends Can Be Murder
Weddings Can Be Murder
Alibis Can Be Murder
Escapes Can Be Murder
Old Bones Can Be Murder
Sweethearts Can Be Murder
Money Can Be Murder
Road Trips Can Be Murder
Cruises Can Be Murder (coming soon!)
Holidays Can Be Murder - a Christmas novella

The Samantha Sweet Series
Sweet Masterpiece
Sweet's Sweets
Sweet Holidays
Sweet Hearts
Bitter Sweet
Sweets Galore
Sweets Begorra
Sweet Payback
Sweet Somethings
Sweets Forgotten
Spooky Sweet
Sticky Sweet
Sweet Magic
Deadly Sweet Dreams
The Ghost of Christmas Sweet
Tricky Sweet
Haunted Sweets
Spellbound Sweets – a Halloween novella
The Woodcarver's Secret – prequel to the series

The Heist Ladies Series
Diamonds Aren't Forever
The Trophy Wife Exchange
Movie Mogul Mama
Homeless in Heaven
Show Me the Money

Children's Books
Daisy and Maisie and the Great Lizard Hunt
Daisy and Maisie and the Lost Kitten

Made in United States
Orlando, FL
08 October 2023

37684759R00171